Amy and the Fox

John Lake

Published by Armley Press 2015

Acknowledgements

Layout: Ian Dobson
Design: Mick Lake
Cover art: Chris Fairbairn
Everything else: Mick McCann

Visit:
rookerygallery.com
armleypress.com

For Jo, who followed her heart and it led her to me.

ISBN 978-0-9934811-0-9

1

An instant of panic—
> Dislocation: of thoughts from feelings.
> From reason.
> The car sidewinding into the wrong lane to miss the thing in the road. Amy's gaze snatched away from the slipstream of French pastureland and squeezed ahead – locked – down a tunnel of potential death.
> Another car approaching too fast...
> Their rental car slaloms back across the painted centre line to the imagined safety of the conventional world, collision smoothly avoided.
> Amy grapples with the seatbelt to look back and glimpse a shape on the crown of the road. A rusty blur; is it moving? Then – gone, wiped away by a stand of trees in the bend of the road as distance and perspective play their work.
> Colin is pushing back up through the gears. He rolls his shoulders, fully in control of the wheel. The emergency manoeuvre around the object – was it a fox? – barely registered on his emotional radar.
> She watches him check the rearview mirror.
> 'What was it?' she says.
> 'Dead fox, by the looks of it. Came out of a blind spot. Caught me by surprise.'
> The diction clipped: his adopted form of speech in tight spots. Military-like, even though he's never served – a kind of code for the abnegation of the emotional self in the matter. Shit happens, so deal with it. From his father, though he'd deny it.
> 'Are you sure it was dead? I thought I saw it move.'
> 'If it's not dead it's because I didn't just kill it.'
The witticism raises no laugh. She's thinking about the fox – about going back. He can tell, of course he can.
'Someone else had already hit it,' he says.
> 'I know. I know it wasn't you. You're too good.'
He wonders if she means his driving skills or his morals.
> 'I'm sure it was dead, love. I got a pretty good look at it.'
> 'I know. I know you did, Sweetie.'
> They fall silent by common consent.

Amy's mind latches onto the pet name she just called him. It started as a joke – a line from a film they saw together a whole marriage ago. *Sweetie* – she called him it in a bad Chicago accent once, and now it's naturalised into their relationship. She mimics the patronising tone from the girl in the film. It's meant as an intimacy but sometimes raises eyebrows at dinner parties. She wonders if that ever bothers him. Is he really comfortable with it or does he hate her every time she uses it in public? Does he even notice?

The swerving of the car to miss the dead fox in the road and the flashback to the cosy world of London dinner parties buffet one another in her mind, two winds meeting from different emotional directions. In the turbulence, her eyes dance around the car and grab a snapshot of her husband's profile. His gaze is fixed on the road, his facial muscles at rest, uncalled upon to give expression; a thoroughly pragmatic face.

She pictures the road behind – an apparition of an injured animal limping across the highway. And she pictures the road ahead, the shrinking miles drawing them on to the thing above the gorge.

All these hours, these days, of staring at motion are driving her a little mad. In London they only ever drive to the supermarket, and even then only if they've forgotten to order an Ocado delivery.

Her flitting sight settles on the dashboard; she switches on the radio. A male voice speaks in French. She isn't in the mood to concentrate and have to translate. She pulls a CD from the pile Colin thought to bring. It's one of hers. Robert Palmer. Colin must have packed this for her. The thought cheers her up. She pushes it into the slot and skips to 'Addicted to Love'. When the music crashes in over the drum intro, Amy Trent laughs:

'Ha.'

'What?'

'Nothing ever freaks you out, does it?' she says over the music.

'What d'you mean?'

'I've been driving for as many years as you but that would've freaked me out. Specially with the left-hand drive. I'd've bumped right over it and probably crashed into a ditch.'

'It's just alert driving, that's all. You'd've reacted just the same.'

While she watches him speak, his fringe stirs in a draught from the ventilator. Underneath she sees the tiny, white worm of a forehead scar from his old kendo practice, fooling about afterwards with the masks off. Her mind falls into its old routine of ticking off his other war wounds: the scar on his left lower leg from motocross, a dodgy knee from a skiing accident and a chronically weakened right shoulder socket from an awkward hang-gliding moment. Boyish fads and phases he's gone through. Battle scars he bears cheerfully without regret.

'Yeah, but you don't get freaked out – not by anything,' she says.

'What d'you mean? I do. I get freaked out by stuff.'

'I mean, what about that time in Kenya? When that crocodile crawled out from under that bush.'

'I was freaking out.'

'You didn't show it though.'

'Ah, but you admit I was freaking out.'

'I only know that because you said so.'

'Just because I'm freaking out doesn't mean I have to look like I'm freaking out. I suppose there's a part of me that thinks looking like you're freaking out is uncool. No, delete that. Not uncool. It's unnecessary. In fact, it's counter-productive.'

'Oh yeah? Well it still didn't stop you tossing and turning all night last night.'

'Oh, right,' says Colin, twigging on to the real subject. 'That's what this is all about.'

'All what?'

'All this freaking out business. You're freaking out about the jump.'

Amy sees no point denying it.

'Are you kidding? I'm bricking it. I had dreams about it all night. And don't tell me you didn't.'

She can tell by the way his mouth opens and closes, like a carp at the surface of a truth, that he isn't going to admit it.

'You *know* it's gonna be tops,' he says. 'Remember that time parascending in Morocco. You *loved* that.'

This was schoolboy Colin speaking now, familiar to her from stories his brother used to tell about him. Col the Fearless, climber of any tree, scaler of any wall and leaper from the highest heights.

9

When he dreams of jumping, he's Tarzan.

When Amy dreams, it's the opening scene from *Cliffhanger*.

'Parascending is not the same thing,' she says. 'You descend slowly, for a start.'

'It'll be a breeze. Just start your yoga breathing before you jump and close your eyes as you let go. We talked about this – remember?'

'I know, I know. But still. You're better at these things. Like – your skydiving and your kendo and – all that stuff. The most daring thing I ever do these days is my aerobics class.'

'Exactly. You're in shape. Up to the challenge. Anyway, you *are* daring. What about diving in the Seychelles? There were sharks around, remember? And what about skiing? People die skiing. Look at Sonny Bono.'

He had to go and use the 'D' word.

Amy respects Colin's rejection of superstition, but still she hates to tempt fate, or anyone to.

Colin is able to use reason to banish fear. His faith in reason is the thing she most admires in him, and most despises. Reason: the religion of robots. When she sees it surface in him, she's both inspired and frustrated. It makes her feel that her own grasp on reason is tentative, needing the safety net of something mystical and unaccountable.

But she's thirty-six and about to do her first bungee jump, and fear feels very rational. Just thinking about it triggers an adrenaline rush of anticipated freefall. She can't stop thinking about the height. Then the drop – looking down into it; being made to look down. She imagines a male instructor's big, gloved hand at the base of her skull, tilting her forward over the chasm. Perched on an iron bridge spanning a 200-foot-deep gorge. Waiting to tumble into the dreadful, gaping, dizzy space below. Waiting for that hand to slap her on the back...

Good to go.

'Look,' says Colin.

He nods at the horizon.

'You can see the foothills. Nearly there. Making good time.'

He looks pleased.

She knows he loves this kind of stuff but does he have to

look so pleased?

2

They came to France for a week to travel the southern littoral in a Hertz car, camp site to camp site, with a tent from Colin's student days rolled up in the boot. They discovered it to be embarrassingly out of date; it took an age to pitch, while all around them the other campers' dome-frames sprang up in seconds. The first stiff breeze blew off the mustiness of years in a dark cupboard, though, and, put to the test, it stayed upright and could hold off a light squall.

A slack period in Colin's work had coincided with a school holiday so the trip was a rush decision. Colin suggested camping after a handful of website hits produced only fully booked hotels. It would be fun, he said, and Amy understood without having to be told that he wanted to prove they were both still young enough to rough it. It freed them from the bind of reservations connecting like dots along a fixed, timetabled route, so Amy was happy to go along with the idea as long as it didn't involve days in the rain. Wet family summers camping in the Cotswolds as a teenager had taught her where to draw the line.

'If it rains I'm going to a hotel,' she told him bluntly. But it didn't much, and after the second night sleeping fitfully on the lilo she began to consider lying about what the French weather forecaster was saying on the radio. Until she got used to it, the risk of a small fib seemed worth it for a night in a comfy bed. But she stuck it out and it never came to that.

When Colin saw the bungee company's poster in a bar in St Tropez she knew there'd be no stopping him. He asked if she minded, and she didn't want to mind, so she said no. She told him it was something she'd always been curious about. He said it looked like a thrill, and it was only an hour's detour from the motorway route back north.

But now that the reality is upon her it's too much. Recurring thoughts of the drop are consuming her mind. She's fine with heights on buildings or cliffs so long as there's a barrier, so what's the problem?

But she already knows: she's scared of making a fool of herself. In her mind, after the vision of the drop, comes the sight of herself panicking, refusing to do it, growing hysterical, punching the attendants in her frantic retreat from the edge.

And squashed beneath that is the fear of an accident. In Grasse, she sacrificed a sunny morning to checking the company's safety specs in an internet café. She learned how the back-up fall-arrest system operates, and what substance is used to protect the rubber cord from UV and ozone deterioration. At the time, she was reassured. But now that crunch time is approaching, it feels more dreamlike as it gets more real, and the dream-logic is focusing her mind on the central moment. The leap. The moment of letting go. Letting go of control. In that moment of breaking contact with a solid object you relinquish control of reality and reality has control of you. Perhaps that's what she's really afraid of: the deeply rooted reality, the quiddity, of the experience.

'What's he saying to them?' Colin asks her.

They're on the bridge among a loose scrum of people waiting to be rigged up for their jumps. A young attendant – a tall, loose-limbed, young Frenchman, long and lean in a blue one-piece flying suit with a beard from his student days that he's never had to shave off – is working his way down the straggle of clients, going through their briefings. He has the running order and everybody's details written down from when they signed in.

Amy is trying to catch his French as a way of distracting herself from the void of the gorge all around them. The sky is overcast here and she's glad of it. Sunshine would bring too much clarity. She doesn't want clarity right now. Not anymore. She wants the whole thing to pass in a grey blur and be over with.

'Stuff you'd expect,' she says. 'How much do you weigh? Any health problems? You're not pregnant, are you?'

'I wish I was. I'd earn a bloody fortune in the circus.'

'Only in the nineteenth century, Sweetie, or possibly Romania. Are they in the EU?'

'I mean the media circus.'

Amy keeps her gaze fixed on Colin. The views are wonderful really, her eye corner has already caught the white rope of river at the bottom, but she'll face them when she has to.

'What's she waiting for?' Colin says.

His eyes are on the woman on the platform – preparing to jump, like a diver about to poise on a poolside board. His question isn't impatience, it's curiosity.

The attendant gets to them. His flight suit bears a company logo and a label with the name 'Patrick'. Amy puts Colin's question to him about the waiting woman, adding is there something wrong – hoping to hear that the weather is turning and all jumps are to be called off through no one's fault, least of all hers. They'll have to abandon the idea and push on north. They have to get back to work – Colin's interviewing David Cameron for *The Independent* the day after tomorrow and she has to be back at school on Monday.

'Ah, this is routine, nothing to be concerned about,' Patrick explains in French, making her heart drop. 'My colleague at the top must wait for the all-clear from my other colleague at the bottom. We have to make sure that the conditions are right before each jump. Sometimes we have to wait a short while for his signal, that's all.'

Before she can ask what kind of conditions – it isn't windy and visibility is OK – Colin asks her what he's saying. It's a question she's heard too many times over the past fortnight and irritation prickles her.

'Sorry, monsieur. I didn't know you don't speak French,' Patrick says in English to Colin. 'You've done this before?'

'Not exactly. Stuff like it.'

'My husband's done skydiving,' says Amy, obeying an irrational urge to broadcast that they are married; as if that might make the world love them more.

'Ooh la la,' says Patrick, perhaps a touch sarcastically. She didn't think anybody really said that – it makes him appealingly camp and tickles her. 'But you know,' he continues, 'this – there's nothing like it. The bungee? Nothing like it. For me it is the best thrill. I was one of the pioneers in this country. The Club Elastique de France. Three of us died in one year testing this sport.'

Amy shudders: the 'D' word again.

'Not me, of course,' he concludes. Colin laughs appropriately and she makes a brave face of chiming in with it. 'Safety 'as improved much since those days. That was in 1989. Sometimes at the end of the drop we woul go 'eadfirst into the water practically up to the waist. What a buzz!'

1989. He doesn't look old enough. Maybe bungee jumping keeps him youthful, constantly reborn upside down out of the ecstasy of gravity. Her yoga teacher maintains that headstands are good for the heart and resisting the aging process.

'I've seen that here today,' says Colin perkily. 'You still do that. I've seen people getting their hair wet.'

'You think you'd like that?'

'Yeah. Could probably do with a hair-wash. Been on the road for two weeks.'

'Camping,' Amy says helpfully, when what she wants to say is *Col, what are you doing?*

But of course he knows what he's doing. When his head touches the river at the end of the drop, that's when his emotions will come alive.

A walkie-talkie in Patrick's hand emits an electric gargle then some tinny words.

'Ah, here she goes,' he says.

They've got the all-clear. Amy has to look, and moves closer to the parapet, but keeping her eyes from glancing down.

The jumper stretches her body in a cruciform as perfect as Christ on Sugarloaf Mountain, then tilts forward while bending her knees so that she's already leaning out over the chasm when her feet push her off the edge. Free of the touch of the bridge, she curves her spine concavely and swan-dives away at the optimum angle. As the girl plummets toward the zenith, Amy has to turn away, suddenly dizzied. Screams and whoops of delight echo up the sides of the gorge. The river is so far below as to be just a murmur, like distant traffic from their London bedroom at night.

'Justine is a regular,' says Patrick. 'Very experienced. And what about you, madame? Your first time?'

Amy nods.

'You see what she did there? When you jump, you push yourself away from the bridge so the cord runs out straight behind you, like a jet stream. Not directly above you like a parachute. If the cord follows you out like that it will give you a smooth ride like a swing when you come back up.'

She's tried to avoid thinking about the upswing. *Thanks, Patrick, good job.*

'If the cord drops straight down, the ride can be a little sudden. Nothing to worry about, you understand. The elasticity of the cord makes everything OK. A slow, steady stretch. No

15

whiplash. One thing you must remember. Whatever 'appens, do not touch the cord. Don't try to take 'old of the cord. If you're turning over in the air, leave the cord alone. Stay out of its way. You don't need to do anything. When you come back up, keep your arms in like this.' He shows them how, hugging himself. 'The cord and the 'arness will do all the work for you. You both got that?'

'Yes,' she finds herself saying in unison with Colin, like attentive toddlers in nursery school. She wants to say more, feels a need to remonstrate, explain what's on her mind; but it's a mood, not a thought, and it will not take expression. Instead she says, 'Then what happens?'

'I don't understand.'

'At the bottom. How do we get off?'

'You can see for yourself,' says Patrick, pointing toward the parapet.

'I haven't looked yet.' She makes a point of looking only at Patrick until he understands that she doesn't want to look over the parapet.

'Of course,' he says, glancing apprehensively at her husband. 'I will explain. After you stop swinging, the cord will lower you down and my colleagues down below catch it with a hook and bring you safely to the riverbank.'

Hanging upside down, she thinks, like a kipper. Actually, that bit doesn't sound too bad. She likes the idea of being brought safely to the riverbank. It sounds romantic and comforting. She imagined they'd have to winch her all the way back up to the bridge just to add more torture.

'Don't we get a flying suit?' she says.

'These are just our uniforms. For the company.' He points the walkie-talkie antenna at the logo on his chest. 'Jeans and T-shirts are fine as you are. If you get a little chilly on the way down, believe me, you are going to be too busy 'aving fun to notice it.'

Again she feels the impulse to remonstrate, perhaps against the certainty of his trite prediction. She wonders if any of the other waiting jumpers is feeling the same emotions and thinking the same thoughts as her. Everyone looks relaxed but she supposes she looks relaxed too. How many of them are struggling to keep their composure, meekly following a code of behaviour imposed on them by the Age of Reason many centuries ago?

Useless thoughts continue to buzz like wasps in her head as they wait their turn to have the ankle and body harnesses and carabiners fitted.

Oh. Who's going to go first? They haven't thought about that; she hasn't thought about that. At least she isn't dwelling on the drop now. Her spirit backs farther away from that the more her body approaches it. Is this what it's like to be a zombie?

'OK,' says Patrick, returning to them at last. 'Which one of you is going to go first?'

'Amy?' says Colin.

The phrase *I'll go first* comes into her mind from *The Weakest Link*, addiction to which is a hazard of working school hours close to home.

'You go first.'

'Are you sure? Don't want to get it over with?'

'Yes, really. I'm sure. If you can do it, I can do it. Besides, I want to watch you do it, and once I'm down there I'll probably be so excited I'll forget to look up.'

'If you're sure.'

'I'm sure. Off you go. And don't do anything daft.'

A flight-suited official helps Colin get ready while another checks and adjusts the equipment. 'What are you,' she hears him ask Colin in English, 'ninety kilos?'

'Spot on.'

'And Patrick says you like to dip in the water, yes?'

'Yes,' he says, sending Amy the thumbs up.

Amy tries to look at the gantry to work out how the safety line pays out and how it's all anchored to the bridge, the kind of detail Colin will be able to recall later, but there's too much to take in and none of it's staying in. She keeps remembering a line from a journalist's account that she read on the internet back in Grasse: 'There was plenty of time to think about death but not enough time to do anything about it.'

Stop it, she tells herself. It's like Colin says. It'll be a breeze. It'll be tops.

It looks like they're ready for the jump. Colin smiles and shouts, 'See you on the riverbank,' as he shuffles out onto the platform like a prisoner in shackles, his free hands clasping the rails to either side.

It's a steel platform bracketed to the bridge structure underneath, the surface studded for sureness of grip, and about two feet square. That much she does notice, the way she notices things like sacrificial altars in museums. One step remains between her husband and the sky gods below.

As he waits for the all-clear, looking straight ahead towards the low hills on the horizon beyond where the river alters its course and passes from view, he lets go of the rails. The man in charge is at the gate to the platform with a hand stretched out, resting lightly on Colin's shoulder, like the priest officiating at the offering; Colin, spine perfectly upright, a model in profile of homo sapiens, stands palms against thighs as if at attention.

Amy doesn't know how he can bring himself to do that. Even though she now accepts her fate and will do it herself in a few moments, she still won't know how he did it and stayed calm. Bothered, maybe, but not letting it bother him. No temptation to bend the knees for that extra groundedness that she knows she will be striving for, that she is even now unconsciously striving for on his behalf. No temptation to look down or close his eyes. No temptation anymore to look at her. Living purely, rationally – privately – in the moment.

That is the part of him that she will never understand and will never know.

The all-clear comes over the walkie-talkie.

'Now I'm going to count down from five, OK?' says the official. 'And to improve your language skills, I'm going to do it in French. Cinq, quatre, trois, deux, un... allez!'

Colin jumps on cue with no hesitation, as she knew he would. The take-off isn't as graceful as the girl's earlier. He gets the knees right but his arms, though stretched out, come up too high above his head in a slack, asymmetrical V – the old shoulder wound. He seems to get the angle pretty well, flying down the curve of a parabola that will reach its cusp midstream over the river. As he dives through the void his howl of approval reverberates back up from the deep distance.

This time she doesn't look away; she wants to watch him all the way down, all the way to the surface of the river. She's even able to see a twist of foamy water slide off his hair as the contracting cord begins to pull him up and swing him under the bridge and out of sight.

But he isn't holding his arms in like they were told to. What's he playing at?

She's so caught up in the moment now she's leaning out over the parapet, waiting for him to emerge, when the jump official's walkie-talkie barks its horrible noise.

There he is again going back down, but bobbing like a rag doll. *Mind the cord!* she thinks as it jumps around him. His arms look loose, dancing to their own tune. Why isn't he keeping them pulled in? She notices the team far below on the riverbank dashing about like disturbed ants and can hear their tiny voices over the sound of the water's passage – Lilliputians shouting. She turns around. Something is happening up here, by the platform. Activity; raised voices. The French cuts through into English in her brain.

'Lower the cable, but gently. Something's wrong. They need to pull him in quickly.'

'What's wrong?' Amy says, moving towards the open gate in the barrier. 'Qu'est ce qui se passe?'

Patrick steps forward, putting a hand on her shoulder to keep her back. 'Madame, please, move back. It's not safe.'

'You said it *was* safe.'

'I mean for you, 'ere. Please.'

She lets him shepherd her back a few feet. 'What's happening? What's happened to Colin?' She can't remember if she's told him their names, though he has them written down. 'What's happened to my husband?'

'We don't know up 'ere yet. We have to wait for what they say on the ground.'

His hands are still on her upper arms. Amy shrugs them away and turns back to the parapet to see. Colin has stopped bouncing; he's low enough for them to hook him in. They cluster round the task, three, four of them, desperate to bring him in. Even from so far away, she can see he isn't moving. He's – dangling, his body utterly at the mercy of sway and momentum. She watches as they lift him to the ground. What else can she do from up here but watch? Then the team are all over him, obscuring him from her view.

She can scream. She can call out his name. He might hear her. He might respond. But if he can't, it will only distract them from doing their job.

'Madame,' says Patrick behind her.

She turns around. 'What happened? Is he OK?' She's all but clamouring at him.

'He is unconscious. An ambulance is on its way.'

'What happened? Was he hurt?'

'It seems that there is a blow to 'is 'ead.'

'But – how? There isn't anything to hit your head on. Just water.' Then she thinks. 'The bridge!'

'It was a clean jump. 'E flew away from the bridge.'

'No. Underneath. Bouncing up.'

Patrick shakes his head. 'It's not possible, madame.'

'Why not?'

'Believe me, madame, we know. It's physics. It's not possible. If it was, we wouldn't do it. It would be too dangerous. It would be madness.'

'Well something must've done it.'

'I know, madame, and per'aps soon we will know. But now I think I should take you to be with your 'usband.'

He's right. What's she thinking? They can tell her what struck him later. Right now she needs to be with Colin. 'Yes, of course. I'm sorry, Patrick.'

'You know my name.'

'It's on your uniform.'

In the panic, he's forgotten. 'Of course. And what should I call you?'

'Amy – Amy Trent,' she adds, catching herself thinking litigiously. Someone has to be at fault here. But they have it all written down. 'What about our car?'

'We can collect it later. Now we should 'urry.'

Within minutes they're scrambling into a vehicle, the jump operation shutting up shop behind them, then speeding away to Colin and hospital. And despite her worry and concern for Colin, still there's a corner of her mind that's relieved – relieved! – that she's going down like this: that she will never have to go down that other way.

3

She never thought he might die. Back there, up on the bridge. After the accident. Never once did she consider that death – the 'D' word that had so plagued her in the moments leading up to the incident – could be the outcome.

I didn't, she thinks, staring down at the coffin, faced with a different reality now – throwing dirt into her husband's grave.

I didn't. Not once.

It's as far as the thought will go. Beyond that, there's nothing but the wanting him back.

A log in the river. That's what they said. They found tree splinters in the head wound afterwards. One of the 'conditions' the team on the riverbank were there to check for: one they missed, or failed to spot in time.

No one has unequivocally told her if anyone saw the log or if it's simply the most plausible theory. The inquest back in France is still pending; her lawyers are on the case. Not her doing really. Edward, Colin's father, has done all the donkey work – studying the relevant documents, making the necessary phone calls. It's his way of being useful, keeping himself busy, but he's doing it for her more than anyone.

A log. A meeting of two fast-moving objects at a fleeting point in time. The only possible time – measurable in perhaps only hundredths of a second – when the two things could have collided. Two objects incapable of occupying the same space at the same time. Mass meeting mass, releasing destructive energy. A window of time only describable in any human terms as an instant. Not the instant of death: that would come later in the ambulance with her watching helplessly as the paramedics scrambled at their work – a confused moment of shock and awe ending in flatline.

He never woke up, though he'd seemed stable. 'Heart failure' it reads in French on the death certificate, before noting the contributory circumstances.

Every death is a failure of the heart.

Later, a week maybe, after she'd absorbed the devastation of loss – when she felt it wearing off, when she was most afraid of losing the wordless, comforting numbness that kept her cocooned from reality while family and friends fretted around her taking care of her needs – she placed the blame on the gate official. If only he hadn't delayed the jump with his stupid joke about testing Colin's French; a second would've done it. If only he'd counted down from three instead of five. Two numbers, maybe even one, fewer and their life together would have continued, undisturbed.

Later still, as the details dissolved and then reconfigured in her memory, she repositioned the blame on someone else. One of the earlier jumpers took too long dithering on the platform. That regular, what was her name? Monique, or... oh, something fucking French.

Then the scenario morphed again, seen from another ingenious perspective, into a different set of circumstances throwing light on a new instrumental detail. And so the exhausting round of rewriting history continued until, finally, she blamed herself.

If she'd just gone first without all the chit-chat, without those precious milliseconds of stupid mind-trash about *The Weakest Link*. Then nobody's head would have been in any water near any log.

She began to worry that this was just the start of a lifetime – what remained of it – of what-ifs. So many events could have intervened to delay or expedite the timing of the fatal moment. Even understanding that these events could be linked back to the dawn of time didn't help: the what-ifs kept coming. What if they'd been one position in front or behind in the queue of waiting jumpers? What if they'd had to stop for petrol or ask for directions on their way there?   What if they'd taken the time to make love that morning before driving to the gorge? She went on replaying it, searching for a way for Colin to reach the end of the drop outside that window – that narrow archer's slit – of time, and the driftwood to miss him, if only by inches, as he bobbed out of its path, wet-headed and elated, then happily boring everyone with the tale at dinner parties forever after: 'I saw it, it was *this* close; damn thing nearly had my eye out.' She can just hear him.

He could have missed that instant. He should have missed it. That's what he'd always been so sure of. It was the phlegmatic core of his belief – his world's foundation: that vast statistical margin of improbability which virtually ensured survival. But there's one statistic that the people in Colin's rational world overlook – the one they skate over with the word 'virtually'. After all the calculated reasoning that he believed the nature of reality demanded, in the end it was the virtual world that caught him out.

But what about her – didn't she miss it too, back there on the bridge? After the fatal instant. (She resists calling it the fateful instant.) She knew there was something wrong: she could see he wasn't conscious. But it was Colin, gung-ho, unfazable, battle-scarred, indestructible Colin, and they'd told her the ambulance was coming and she was being driven to his side, driven by responsible people with a professional concern and involvement, and she knew that when she got there, when she reached him, he'd already be laughing it off, nothing but a bump on the head, don't know what all the fuss is about, and she was so relieved that she would never have to jump herself that she didn't think for once that he might be dead, not once.

She is back at the end point again; but this time she steps beyond.

'I'm sorry,' she whispers down into the grave.

She looks up to see if anyone on the other side has seen her mouth the words but they're all lost, eyes downcast, in their own grief, or comforting those close by them. Christine, his mother, sobbing into the crook of her husband's shoulder, her clutched black hat lifted in two white-knuckled hands, grown knobbly with age and gardening, to shut out the inconceivable sight of her dead son's coffin in front of her. His gaze, Edward's, her husband's, Colin's father's, sombrely locked on the coffin. A quiet, uncharacteristic tear trickles down the creases of his face past the military tip of his white moustache, and becomes lost in his wife's grey hair. Next to them but apart, alone, Max, Colin's younger brother, their one remaining child. Amy hasn't seen him in years. His hair is still long and unkempt, the way he's worn it forever. His black tie is a narrow, parallel-straight strip – a throwback to the Eighties, when it would probably have had piano keys on it. He looks – lost, awkwardly and awfully lost, his eyes wide and quivering as if trying to view steam through fog. Not weeping, just staring. Unable to blink, unable to look away, connected like his father to the coffin, only the coffin.

None of them deserve this, she thinks with an irreconcilable pang of guilt.

Amy can see that none of them saw her lips move or overheard her apology, nor any of the mourners standing behind them. No one is going to ask what she's sorry for and create a scene around the grave. They're all busy with their own sorries and their own sorrow. Every death is a failure of many hearts.

Her own family stands with her on this side of the grave: her mother and father, still and solemn. Mum is wearing her tragic, noble stiff upper lip, the one she usually reserves for Remembrance Sundays. Dad's face bears the melancholy, sympathetic frown that shaggy eyebrows and long eyelashes can give a man, an expression that's a palimpsest behind any other expression. A surge of love glows in Amy's heart towards him, but stubbornly refuses to enfold her mother. Alice and Stuart, her sister and brother-in-law, down from Norwich, are standing a pace or two behind her parents, but not the children: they didn't bring them – it's better, they're too young; she'll see them soon enough.

An agreed, natural division has fallen between the two families, one either side of the grave. People need to be with those who need them; this is not the time to mingle. Their mutual loss is enough to bridge the chasm in the ground between them. In the chapel, before they transported him down to this hole that will be his final home and might one day be hers, a lay preacher performed a humanist service. Instead of souls and angels, it was consciousness flowing into a sea of universal energy, nothing about God; a bit quasi-Buddhist. She knew it was what he wanted – they'd talked about these things – so she'd insisted on it. No one had put up a fuss. No one wanted to disrespect his wishes, nor voice their private objections. At the chapel, they played the mourners in with Whitney Huston singing 'The Greatest Love of All'. It was the one song she remembered him saying he wanted at his funeral – a strange choice, not a song she liked, and brazen, considering the lyrics were about self-love, but it was what he wanted, and it reflected his sense of humour. Afterwards, the congregation filed out to 'Vienna' by Ultravox, which she chose: a song he loved about a city they both loved. The absence of religion from the service, however, rang pointless among the attendant crucifixes and stained-glass windows. In the end, there had been compromise after all. But she didn't feel bitter and she hoped Colin wouldn't have.

She could've held back the tears, she could hold them back now if she wanted to. She's had two weeks of tears already. A wet fortnight. But she let them come. It was something everyone expected. Her grief united them; their grief converged in the sharing of hers. She was the centre that was expected not to hold. She let the tears come, though she knew they would make her feel no better.

She crouches to the ground, places a kiss on a bunch of flowers and drops them into the grave. She can smell the loamy dampness of the earth. It rained last night. She hears birds too. Singing. It sounds inappropriate: the indifference of the real, living, eternal world invading their thanosphere of bereavement.

The mourners begin a slow procession round the hole, moving cumbersomely, like a shackled chain gang, their gestures of goodbye stifled by the hopelessness we feel at the waste of a foreshortened life. Amy steps out of the way, taking her tears to her father's bosom. It's always her father she takes them to. As they file past her, it strikes her how many people are here for Colin. So many friends, and so many good friends; she'd forgotten how many. She never tried to count them, not even leafing through her address book. Who managed to contact them all? So many more now out here than were at the service inside, where only a few faces, peripheral blurs, had half-registered as she walked into the chapel. Her first time down the aisle on her father's arm – they wedded in a Registry Office.

One by one they turn towards her, heads bowed, ritually lifting her their sympathy in a deferential nod or a shake of the hand, some of them looking up to hug and kiss her. Good friends from work, her fellow teachers; Colin's journalist friends and colleagues – some familiar, some not – solemn, polite, restraining their impatience to check their texts; close friends from down the years. Some faces only recognisable from a distant past, startling her towards memories she can't chase right now, names she can't place. Old friends of his from school and university, players from a history that is already dissolving. In one sense, they reassure her: their presence, their mourning, the charitable gift of their remembering. In another, they terrify her: what is she going to say to them all when the moment comes for her to speak?

The procession goes on, so many, and after a while and without knowing how or why, she finds herself looking for that one face that shouldn't be there. The woman alone whom no one else seems to know or, if they do, won't look at. Doesn't every husband's funeral have one? She imagines a lone, keening figure standing off at a guilty distance, but when Amy looks for her she isn't there. She doesn't know whether to be happy or disappointed. She isn't happy; she isn't disappointed.

The last of the gatherers are plodding wordlessly up the churchyard slope towards the gravel drive along which their vehicles are parked. As they shuffle away up the hill, she feels her father squeeze her shoulder gently.

'Come on, love.'

The world has shrunk back to the six of them; even Alice and Stuart have gone on. Then Edward and Christine stir, she unsteadily, half destroyed, brought to ruin, he supporting her and offering stiff bolts of encouragement, willing some of his strength to seep into her through the press of their bodies. He smiles sadly across the grave at her, and his eyes briefly take in her mother and father behind her before he helps his wife away.

'Come on, love,' her father says again. There is a comfort in the repetition, the words reaching more gently into the folds of her muffled consciousness. 'Let them do their job.'

That puzzles her at first. Them? Her mind tries to hunt down a religious allusion. Angels, perhaps? It isn't like her father. Then she notices the gravediggers with their shovels standing a few discreet yards off under a tree, and her mind flashes on a scene from Shakespeare.

Her mother links her father's arm with a stately shake of the head that asks little more than what the world is coming to.

With one last look at the coffin, Amy turns away and accompanies her parents up the hill toward the business of the wake and what she will say to everyone. She hears the shovels stabbing into the heaps of earth but she doesn't look back.

She mustn't look back.

4

It's in the upstair room of the Nestler's Arms, the pub that dominates the main street of the local village. She doesn't know what to call it. 'Reception' makes it sound like a wedding. She thinks she prefers 'wake'. She prefers not to think of it at all.

They decided among them, she and his parents, to bury him here near his family home. They, Edward and Christine, have their obvious reasons, and she – well, it will give her an incentive to go on visiting them, though she'll never put it to them that way. She doesn't want to lose touch with them, of course not, never, but instinctively she wants contact on her terms. She knows it's stubborn and wilful and horrible but it's a side of herself she indulges for what she believes are good reasons. She's her mother's daughter in that way, at least. The last thing she wants is to remain attached to them by grief alone, then later by habit, and finally by duty and guilt. But she can imagine herself stoically trilling 'Is it all right if I come over this weekend?' down the phone to them from time to time. To visit them. To visit the grave. Colin's grave.

My husband's grave.

'That was a lovely announcement in *The Times*,' a woman in a twin-set with matching pillbox hat and pearl-embroidered handbag is saying to Edward. She doesn't know Amy is within earshot. 'Very moving. And all the obituaries were so very kind. What a dreadful loss. Such a talented young man. But with talent comes recklessness. That's my theory. There must be a certain amount of recklessness for talent to succeed today.'

What does she mean, recklessness? Is that supposed to imply that it was his own fault?

Amy is sticking close to Dad, who's moving towards Edward. She's met the woman before somewhere that she can't be bothered to recall right now. She remembers she was vile, but not her name, or where exactly. An old harridan. Thick, matronly make-up then; thick, matronly make-up now.

'Oh, Amy,' the woman wails at her as they approach.

'Stephen,' says Edward curtly – not shortness, just the army still left in him.

Stephen. Her dad's name. She forgets. Steve. That

always makes her giggle, to think of him as a Steve. But not now.

'Edward,' returns her dad, mimicking Edward's vernacular badly, bless him. Never Ted. That will never do. Or Teddy.

The giggles threaten her again.

Stop it!

'I'm so sorry, my darling,' says the woman, pouting vermillion lipstick at her and taking hold of her hands and pushing them together in prayer.

'Thank you,' Amy murmurs, tugging her hands away.

That's all she's said to anyone since she got here.

'What an awful thing to happen!'

Amy says nothing, cannot—

'What an awful way to end your holiday!'

Amy tries to grin. The only reason she can think of to grin is to deflate this dreadful woman's trite, patronising outrage at the dolorous whims of fate. But really, she's gritting her teeth. *It's not fate, you stupid old hag, it just happened. That's what I have to keep telling myself. Shit happens.*

'Excuse me,' she says, the second thing she's said, and turns away.

'Are you OK, love?'

Her dad trails after her. Trails: she doesn't even want him now. All she wants is to hide. Her eyes dart around, looking for caves in the cliffscape of bodies around her. If she keeps her head down she can mole her way in where no one will find her.

'Amy.'

Too late. There he is, standing in front of her like a sudden wall in a cartoon. Richard Something-she's-forgotten. Dickie. Colin's boss – one of them. Reviews editor or something for *The Independent*. They've met a few times. Colin got friendly with him when he was having a mid-life crisis. She doesn't know which one. Dickie thrives on mid-life crises. In fact he gives her the creeps.

She smiles a melancholy smile, saying nothing.

'Amy, I'm so, so sorry.'

She's reminded of the phrase 'dripping with sincerity'. Like treacle. Like Lyons' Golden Syrup, which she's hated since she was a child.

'We're going to miss him at *The Indie*. You know that,

don't you?'

She nods.

'Did you see Toby Young's obituary?'

'I haven't . . . '

'Oh, I'm sorry, darling, of course, of course. All in good time. What was I thinking? Listen, I know it's an old cliché but truly, if there's anything I can do, you will let me know immediately, won't you?'

She nods again. She can feel Dad hovering behind her waiting for an introduction.

'Anything. If you need a good old heart-to-heart, or simply a bit of company in London . . . '

She watches the drink in Dickie's waving hand. This time she doesn't nod.

'Are you all right, Amy?' her dad says.

'Yeah.'

She feels her father's hands at her shoulders, careful, protective, guiding. He smiles at Dickie – all the introduction they're going to get – and she lets him steer her away into a space over by the velvet, drape curtains – how funereal! – being defended by her mother, glass of brandy in hand.

'Let me fetch you a drink,' says her dad. 'What would you like?'

Amy shrugs. It's all she can do. She wants to speak, if only for form's sake, but no words will come.

'Amy, love, you haven't said a word. I know you're upset but you can't go on like this, love. All these people've come not just to see him buried but to celebrate his life.'

He waits for a response but all she can do is look at him. At least she can still look at him.

'He's gone now, love.'

That's it. His voice shivers to jelly. He's pulling her closer so she can't see the rivers of his tears. She puts her arms around him.

'He's buried now, sweetheart,' he squeaks into her shoulder. 'You've got to let go of him and move on. We all have.'

Amy has ended up comforting her father. Over his shoulder, she catches her mother's squirm of discomfort. She's never at home with the intimate variety of strong emotions. Her version of a concerned expression is a fixed thousand-yard stare into the middle distance, like watching over the battlements for the enemy.

Amy wants to say, 'It's already happened, Mother, the enemy's here.'

The enemy is always here, and today it's called death.

At least she's put the brandy down on the table. Her arms are crossed, defensive, unless she's hugging herself, and Mum doesn't do hugs.

'Of course we have,' her mother says, picking up her father's refrain. 'We all have. It's as you say, he's laid to rest now. We must move on. Forward. Amy realises that, don't you, dear?'

She can see her mother's 'concerned' stare morphing by tiny gradations towards inconvenience. She hasn't blinked once. The only thing that moved was her mouth. Amy hates the way Mother calls her 'dear'. She hopes Colin never felt like that about 'Sweetie'.

'I'm sorry,' she says.

She gently prises Dad's head away from her shoulder. She even reaches up and wipes away his tears – something she can't remember ever having done before. A new experience. She wants to suck them off her thumbs.

'I don't want to stay here,' she says, looking from him to her mother, but mostly at him. 'I can't.'

There's no holding back her own tears anymore. They break – then straight away she's snuffling them back up, chided as ever by her mother's put-upon frown which has always worked since childhood not because she's caving in to her mother's incipient threat but because she doesn't want to show weakness to that woman. Something her mother never knew and still doesn't. Something just for her.

'Amy.' She sounds like she's training one of her horses. 'You cannot go. Look at all these people. They're here for you.'

'They're here for Colin.'

'And you, you silly girl.' Not shouting, not making a noticeable scene, but whisper-shouting. Horse whispering. 'They're here for both of you. You can't go now. They've come all this way out of London, most of them, and some of them from much farther afield. Besides, you don't know who might still turn up.'

'Mother, I can't stay, I just can't. I can't talk to any of these people, I can't—'

She looks at her father, his tear-blurred eyes still only inches away from hers.

'I'm sorry, Dad. I just can't do it.'

He closes his eyes and lowers his head – but smiling, accepting.

'I can drive you back if you like.'

Not her dad – a voice from behind her. She turns around and, like another of those cartoon walls, he is there.

Max.

'Mum, Dad, you remember Max. Colin's brother.'

'Max,' says her father, his eyes bulging with the threat of more tears. Somehow they missed each other earlier in the trance of the service. Now they shake hands. 'I don't think we've spoken since Amy and Colin's wedding.'

He's holding it together now, her dad, bolstered by the good happenstance of their reunion after so many years, albeit under such regrettable circumstances. After all, they are family. Or were.

'Mrs Metcalfe,' Max greets her mother.

Amy is impressed that he remembers the family surname, her maiden name.

'Max. Good grief. You look exactly the same,' says Amy's mother.

She sticks out her hand as if to say 'No, no, dear, I don't do kisses' and Max shakes it without missing a beat.

'Max, can you take me home, please?'

Max looks at her parents – a token gesture of seeking their permission.

'Now, please.'

She's desperate to get away from the bustle of carefully negotiated grief and pleasantry around her. She doesn't want it; she can't deal with it. And these people, expecting her to communicate with them on some meaningful level. That's Colin's world, not hers. Colin is happy – was happy – mingling, networking, face-to-facing with people: that was his job. But let her have *her* funeral. The families, yes, but this – she can't face it. She isn't ready.

'Amy,' says her mother, 'I'm not going to beg you. But just think about what you are doing.'

'I have. In fact, I don't have to. I'm sorry, Mum, but I can't. I'll see you both later. Please – say sorry to everyone for me, and thank you. Explain it to them, Dad.'

'I will. Goodbye, love.'

Her dad kisses her forehead.

'Max, look after her, will you? See she gets back all right.'

'I will, sir.'

Max leads her out. She keeps her head down. She makes herself believe no one notices while knowing that everyone is noticing. The widow fleeing from her husband's funeral with his brother. She doesn't care right now. She knows how awful she's being, especially to her friends from work, but she's just relieved to get away. Not from her parents. Or Colin's. She knows she's abandoning them to take the flak. But it's too much. The centre was expected to hold after all, and it didn't. She's confounded their expectations. And although it shames her, she's actually rather proud of it, and she thinks Colin would've been proud of her too.

5

'Max.'

They're in his car – a rental while he's in the country. They escaped without further challenge. The guests will still be expecting her to reappear, thinking she's slipped out to the loo.

'You all right?' Max says.

'I don't wanna go back to my parents'.'

'What do you wanna do?'

'I want to go home.'

'I thought you were staying at your parents'.'

'I mean home home. I mean my home. In London. Mine and Colin's home. I haven't been there for two fucking weeks. Sorry.'

Max's eyes are fixed on the road ahead. The sky is cloudy but there's plenty of day left and the light is good.

'Are you sure?'

'I'm sure.'

'Right, then, hang on.'

He decelerates the car into a U-turn. It's briefly like being on a ride at the fair. The country roads are empty. It's a Friday afternoon. School on Monday, she thinks – her compassionate leave coming to its end.

'Just take me home, please.'

Max checks the dial.

'Lucky for you we've got enough gas.'

Gas. That's new. Where's that come from?

'Just drove up from Glastonbury today.'

Her mind bristles at the remark. Does he think she should feel grateful? It was his brother's funeral. She pushes the thought away. She's being horrid in her self-pity. Of course he was coming up. He would never have missed it.

'What were you doing there?'

'Glastonbury? Visiting some old friends. Thought I might as well while I'm over here.'

Might as well. Shouldn't he have been with his family? His parents? Didn't he think they needed him? She forces her mind to let it go. His relationship with Edward and Christine is none of her business.

'Where are you living now?'

'Tunisia. Got a diving school over there.'

'How long have you been doing that?'

'Three years now.'

'A long time for you. In one place. Must be nice.'

She can't keep track of Max's life. He's been all over the place, done all kinds of jobs, over the last ten years. She isn't in the mood to catch up now though. Whatever he told her about himself, it wouldn't stay in.

They fall into a not uneasy silence for a time. Max knows; he understands. Soon they are on the motorway, the M25, heading back to her quadrant of North London. God, she's missed London.

Max laughs; she detects a noise and it's Max laughing to himself.

'What's funny?'

She isn't offended, just curious.

'You know who they had coming to the reception?' he says, sneaking a mischievous sideways look at her. 'Only David Cameron.'

'What?'

'I think that's what your mum was hinting at before you left. She got my dad to invite him through a Rotary Club mate of his. They were in it together. Your mum and my dad. But why David Cameron, for fuck's sake? I know he's a big man over here, Leader of the Opposition and all that, but what would he be doing at Colin's funeral?'

Amy is still frowning at the idea of her mother and Colin's father colluding behind her back.

'Colin was due to interview him,' she says absently, 'when – when he died. But he wouldn't have wanted him at his wake. Colin hated the Tories. He'll— He'd've gone on supporting Brown to the bitter end.'

'Since when did Colin hate the Tories?' says Max.

The question surprises her – a signifier of how little the brothers knew one another in recent years.

'Since he crept out of the shadow of his upbringing and joined the real world.' Amy bites her tongue but it's too late. Suddenly she's said too much when all day she's been reluctant to say anything at all. 'I'm sorry. I didn't mean that to sound as if

34

I was insulting your parents. I love them, you know. You can love people despite their politics. Relationships don't recognise politics.' She's said too much again. Weak-minded, pseudo-philosophical bullshit. She should keep quiet.

'Go ahead and insult them all you like,' Max says cheerily.

'How come you grew up so different?'

'Different to who? Them or Colin?'

'All of them.'

'I think it's because they sent me away to boarding school. I was the difficult second child they couldn't handle, so they packed me off.'

'Did you hate them for it?'

'Did I or do I?'

'Do you?'

'No. I love them for it. It taught me rebellion and it taught me independence. What more do you need? I hated it at first, obviously, and I suppose I hated them at the time. But at least they weren't there trying to control my life. The way I imagined they were controlling Colin's.'

'Colin did all right,' she says, as though illuminating a truth. 'He turned out just fine.'

'You know, I can barely remember the last time I saw him. Must be two, three years ago.'

'Can we not?' says Amy, putting a stop to it. 'Can we not talk about Colin right now?'

Max looks at her, then back at the road.

'Sure.'

She passes the rest of the journey in silence, watching the traffic and the buildings, the city growing, its environs rising up around them like shapes in a pop video as they trundle deeper into it. She is back in the slow streets of North London, the shops, the pubs, the estate agents, the Tube stations, the news hoardings, all still there, still functioning. Her streets. Colin's streets.

Then they're pulling up in front of the house on their street. Her street. The front door looks intact. It's always the first thing she notices when they get back from a trip. They've been lucky. No break-ins in ten years. She looks around for wood to touch but can't find any near enough.

'D'you want to come in? There isn't any milk but I can nip to the shop. I can offer you a cup of tea. It's up to you.'

'Do you want me to come in?'

Amy says nothing. She isn't looking at him. She's staring at another dashboard of another rental car.

'Would you prefer to be on your own?'

'I think I would.'

'Will you be OK?'

She looks up, reaches across and squeezes the back of his hand.

'Yeah,' she smiles, 'I'll be OK.'

She unhitches the seat belt. Her hand is on the door handle.

'Listen, Max. I wonder if you'd do me a favour.'

'What is it?'

Shrewd Max. Find out first. Don't immediately run with the 'Of course, anything' crowd.

'I wonder if you'd mind stopping by sometime and clearing out Colin's stuff. The stuff in his office. You know. His personal effects. His private stuff. Not clear it out. Not throw it out. More check it out. Look through it for me.'

'Why not you? I'll do it, yeah, but why not you?'

'I don't know, it doesn't feel right. I mean – there might be stuff in there that I don't want to see. That Colin didn't want me to see.'

'What kind of stuff?'

She isn't comfortable with this. She'd drop it now but he said he'll do it already and she can't think of anyone else to ask. Who better than his brother?

'I don't know. Porn. Drugs. Love letters from some old flame. Love letters from some new flame. I couldn't stand it, Max. I couldn't stand it if I came across anything like that. Anything I didn't know about. Anything he didn't want me to know about.'

'Colin wasn't seeing anyone else. I may not've seen much of him over the last ten years but I'd've known if he was being unfaithful to you. I'd've been able to tell. And he would've told me.'

She waits a beat for *And I would've told you* but it doesn't come.

36

'I know,' she says, 'I know I'm being paranoid. If you don't want to do it I won't hold you to it.'

'I've said I'll do it. And I appreciate your concerns. But the idea of Colin two-timing you – that wasn't him.'

'I know. I'm sorry. He's your brother. I'm a bitch.'

'You're not a bitch. You're too soft in the head. When shall I come round? I'm gonna be here for another couple of weeks.'

'The sooner the better.'

'Tomorrow afternoon?'

'That's great. Get it over with before I have to go back to work.'

'Still teaching?'

'Still teaching.'

She's opening the door.

'Sure you're gonna be OK?'

'Positive.'

She climbs out onto the kerb then leans back in.

'Thanks, Max. You're a good friend. Tell them I'm sorry I missed David Cameron.'

'You're not though.'

'No, I'm not. If there's one thing I'm opposed to, it's the Opposition.'

He drives away waving. She waves back until the car is out of sight then turns with her key to face the empty house.

6

It takes her a while to answer the door. In fact it's the sound of the door-bell that wakes her. She's just been with Colin on an adventure in Nigeria. Or was it Kenya? And what was she trying to save him from? The dream dissolves with the harsh clatter of the bell.

She scrambles naked out of bed with no time to brood on the empty side she hasn't slept on all night as she wraps her dressing gown around her and pads down the stairs in her bare feet. It's only midday: she's still wearing her watch from last night. This can't be Max already.

She fumbles at the key in the lock and draws back the bolt and chain, not knowing who it might be – Mormons or anyone.

'Hi.'

It is. Max. She squints past him at the bright daylight beyond, raising an arm to her brow. The movement shifts the front of her dressing gown and she pulls it back across, clutching the collar as if it's winter, not spring.

'God. Sorry. Sorry. When you said afternoon – I wasn't expecting you till later.'

'Hey, no, my bad. I'm used to making an early start, which tends to slide the afternoon forward in the day.'

He wags a finger at her and him.

'We have different ideas of afternoon. I should've thought.'

'Max,' says Amy, knowing he can handle her candour, 'since when did you become so fucking American?'

'If you let me in, I'll tell you.'

He looks different. Different from the last time. When was that? She doesn't mean yesterday at the funeral. Everyone looks the same at funerals. Not the gatherers together but each gatherer separately over time at each subsequent funeral. The same suit or dress comes out, the same gestures, the same awkwardnesses. Mourning doesn't change style with the seasons or the years.

She notices his tan now. She didn't see it yesterday. It's like she didn't see anything all day except the coffin and the grave. Yesterday aside, this is the first time she's seen him since – too long ago.

She excuses herself while she goes upstairs to get dressed. She leaves him sitting at the kitchen table, a neutral space. When she returns, she feels obliged to offer him breakfast.

'No, thanks, I've had breakfast already.'

'I guess you must think this is a bit late for breakfast,' she says, feeling slovenly in her slippers, Primark slacks and a tour T-shirt for a band that was last heard of in the early Nineties.

'It's your home,' says Max. 'Call it brunch.'

'Cup of coffee?'

'That'd be great.'

She turns away to switch the kettle on and he isn't there anymore. She looks out of the kitchen window at the street, at nothing – not even her own reflection in the glass is visible in that bright, dreary light. This is what life will be like now.

'I missed him too by the way,' Max says behind her.

She turns around; he is there again.

'Who?'

'David Cameron.'

'Oh, you went back.'

'I thought it best. Stop tongues wagging.'

She pretends not to notice the implication.

'By the time I got back he'd been and gone.'

'He turned up then.'

'By all accounts. Dad was thrilled. Proud. And your mother.'

'I'm – glad, I suppose. I'm glad I left them to it.'

'Are you going to stay on here?'

'What d'you mean?'

'Are you going to keep the house?'

'Of course. It's my home.'

'I mean you don't feel—'

She lets a pause hang between them. He can't find the words to finish it.

'No. No. It's only been one night but – I dreamed about him.'

'Was he here in the house?'

The question takes her by surprise. Why would he ask that?

'I'm sorry,' she says turning away from him.

She prepares the coffee, hiding in the ritual, seeking the comfort of the ordinary, the teaspoon, the granules – what is it about instant coffee granules? Trying not to let her gaze go back to the window. Max sits silently, his fingertips resting lightly on the surface of the table, still. She can sense his calm, his lack of disquiet, embarrassment or inquisitiveness. He reminds her of Colin in that way, even though they're different in so many others. It isn't their upbringing. It's a centredness in one's own individuality, a level-headedness at the core of the mind and heart. A kind of self-control. She doesn't know if it's a good thing or a bad thing but she knows it's an admirable thing. She wishes she could have some of it right now.

She puts his mug of coffee on the table and the big hand – different to Colin's, rougher, veinier – moves around it.

'So' – she sips at her own drink, though it's too hot – 'Tell me about Tunisia. How did you end up there?'

'Where did we last leave off?'

She looks down, struggling in the riptides of memory, trying to recall the last time the three of them were together, the last time they'd caught up, her focus shredded by a swirl of unwanted images from the past.

Then she smiles in resignation.

'Whatever we talk about there's no way of keeping Colin out of it, is there?'

'Amy, we don't have to talk. I can just get on with it if you'd rather.'

'No. It's just me being silly.'

'It isn't silly to be upset thinking about him. If it is, then I'm silly too.'

'It's a girlie word, isn't it? "Silly". It sounds silly when you say it.'

'Don't be silly.'

They laugh a little; it lightens the mood.

'The last time we saw you, you'd quit land-surveying in Saudi Arabia,' she says, brightening at the anticipation of the family mythology.

'Oman actually, but close.'

'I thought you worked in Saudi.'

'I did. Before Oman. But that's years back. I've seen you

since then.'

'All right, so what happened after Oman?'

'Spain, remember?'

'Oh, that's right. Weren't you working on a building site or something?'

'Christ, I did fucking all sorts in Spain. Building, bar work. Anything I could find.'

'Hang on, what about Thailand? You went to Thailand.'

'That was a holiday. Anyway that was years ago,' says Max dismissively, eager to press on.

'Yeah, after Saudi,' says Amy, slowing him down, a grin spreading across her face as the memory crystallises.

Max closes his eyes. He knows what's coming. Here we go again.

'The hooker story,' says Amy, pointing at him across the kitchen table.

'She wasn't a hooker. That makes her sound awful and she wasn't.'

'You mean it makes it sound sleazy and it was.'

'She was – a companion. A paid companion. I'd been in Saudi Arabia for six months solid and I was single and loaded. I had three weeks before I was going to Oman for another six months, for Chrissake. I didn't have time to meet a so-called nice girl and hope to reach first base.'

Amy laughs.

'There it is again. What the hell is it with all these Americanisms?'

'That's what I was going to tell you. It's Karen. This girl I'm seeing. Living with. She's American.'

'And you've told her that you're American so you have to stay in character to maintain the pretence?'

'Er, no. It's just when you spend a lot of time with someone you start to rub off on each other.'

'Oh, I see,' Amy says in an impressed tone. 'And how much is a lot of time exactly?'

'We live together. We work together. All the time, virtually.'

'How long have you been together?'

'Getting on for two years. Since after I last saw you and Col.' He shrugs. 'You know what I'm like for keeping the folks back home up to speed.'

'So why isn't she here? Didn't she want to come over?'

'She did, but someone needs to run the business. We can't afford to hire anyone else to do it, not yet anyway. We're still building it up. And it's the busy season right now. Besides, she hasn't met the family yet so her absence isn't so bad.'

'You said yet. Sounds as if you're planning for her to meet them. Sounds serious.'

'We'll see. I haven't told them about her yet, so if you don't mind—'

'I won't say a thing,' says Amy and mimes zipping her lips shut. Like in that programme she loved as a child. *Rainbow*. But suddenly his story is at an end and there's nothing to say. She's taken her own promise too literally. It was silly – the girlie word again – and she feels it. Giddy. This is the longest and most diverting conversation she's had with anyone in two weeks. She doesn't know how to deal with it. She feels the onus is on her now to keep it going.

'So what's it like,' she say, mentally unzipping first, 'Tunisia?'

'Can't get a beer after eight o'clock. But Sidi's beautiful. We're not far from there, down the coast.'

'What's Sidi?'

'Sidi-Bou-Said. A quarter overlooking the sea.'

'I've heard of it. Somewhere.' Max's coffee mug is drained, she notices. 'D'you want another?'

He stirs in his seat ever so slightly, just enough to signal restlessness.

'Actually, if it's OK with you, I wouldn't mind getting on with it. I suppose it depends how long you think it'll take.'

'Oh God,' says Amy putting a hand to her lips. 'D'you know how to use a computer?'

'I run a business.'

Amy looks nonplussed as to whether that's a yes or a no. She doesn't know much about them herself. Enough to get by in Word, read emails and connect to the web, mainly for work – she still writes her students' reports by hand.

'I think I'll manage. Listen, Amy, I'm not sure exactly what you want me to do. If there's stuff on the computer, should I wipe it? If there's encrypted stuff, should I tell you about it? I mean what if there's work-related stuff? Shouldn't somebody from Col's work be going through all that?'

'Max, there isn't anyone from work. Or if there is, who? Colin was freelance. He wrote for a number of publications. He didn't have one boss and half those he did have are in competition with one another. But he was a journalist, Max. That's all. He wasn't Tolstoy. He wasn't writing any books, as far as I know. Whatever stories he was working on will be past their sell-by date by now. They died with him.'

'Shouldn't they be passed on to someone?'

'If they're still there after you've finished, I'll look into it.'

'I just need to know where to set the boundaries. How much of him do you want me to erase?'

'Nothing. I don't want you to erase any of him. I don't want you to find anything. But I need you to look.'

'And what if I do find something?'

She gazes at him steadily while her mind boils; she manages to keep her eyes level with his.

'Don't tell me about it.'

Max raises his eyebrows. That's all. He's sat without moving through all this, his stillness resisting the pull of her own edginess, contrasting with it.

'It's a big favour. Keeping it to myself. Do I tell anyone else? Do you trust me not to tell anyone else?'

'As long as I never know, I don't care.'

'Not even if it can damage his reputation? His memory?'

'Of course not. You're his brother. You wouldn't do that. And neither would I.'

He leans forward in the chair now, a prelude to standing.

'I wouldn't. For the record. Tell anyone. If I found anything.' He pauses for emphasis. 'Which I won't. Come on. Show me where I should start.'

'You can start in the office. But actually I want you to search the whole house.'

7

Amy decides to skip making breakfast and go out to the local caff with the paper and the Saturday supplements, getting out of Max's way and leaving him to it. He'll call her on her mobile when he's finished.

Max enters Colin's study. He's never been in it before, it pointlessly strikes him as he steps inside. He remembers a sleep-over in this house once on the couch in the front room (he never did make it as far as his prepared guest bedroom that night) but he never came in this room. All the other times they met up were at other places. They must've been. Though all what other times? There were never that many of them.

Thanks to me.

He doesn't want to think it but his mind forces him to. The blame game.

Everything at a glance looks orderly, manageable – typical Col – and untouched. Amy only returned yesterday. It must be as he left it before they went to France. Papers he was writing, notes, printouts, still litter the desk around the computer. Max slides open the desk drawer and finds a pack of Marlboros. He was sure Col gave up smoking years ago. The pack is still sealed in its plastic wrapping. There for emergencies, a rainy day, perhaps? Or left over from the day he quit?

Max slips them in his jacket pocket and boots up the computer. He spends the best part of an hour skimming through all the files he can access, which is pretty much all of them, nothing encrypted. He sticks at it until he's satisfied that there's no point going on. There's nothing here. Nothing of the sort Amy is worried about, whatever that is exactly. Nothing sleazy, nothing illegal, nothing unfaithful.

A thought occurs to him. If there is encrypted stuff related to work, wouldn't he have it on a laptop? He must have one – he was a journalist. And what about disks, memory sticks? Amy said nothing about any of that. Maybe she's keeping those to herself. And anyway, whether he comes across anything or not that's work-related, then it's irrelevant to his business here, so what does it matter?

He gives up on the PC – this is stupid, he thinks, a more

manly word than 'silly', there's nothing here – and shuts it down. He peruses the bookshelves, reading the spines at an eye-twisting angle. Political stuff. History. Some popular science. Then manuals on writing style and the internet, followed by contemporary novels. What is he looking for? Col wouldn't stack porn on his bookshelves, assuming he had any. It wouldn't fit anyway unless it was that pocket-sized naturist magazine, *Health & Efficiency*. Jeez, does anyone still publish that stuff?

He looks around bewildered for a moment, actually twirling in a circle. There are the CDs and what have you. It all looks like a waste of time. Think. Where would *he* hide something that he wanted out of the path of everyday functional space but still accessible?

He searches the cupboards and drawers, trying to replace everything as it was. A pile of shoe-boxes in a corner catches his attention. He works his way through the first two methodically. One contains a bunch of Col's old photos. Christ, he remembers seeing these years ago. He's in some of them: ancient family snapshots; others, pictures of Col pissed up with the lads at college, and with old girlfriends. He wonders if Amy will want these removed. Nah. She'll have seen them before. They're innocent keepsakes. They represent no harm. The second is a box of negatives. He squints through a couple of strips – it's all temples and mountains and shit – and again thinks he's wasting his time. How long is this going to take, for fuck's sake? He opens the lids of the others in the stack just to say he's checked them. Nothing. That's good, he reminds himself. Nothing is good. He puts it all back the way he found it.

Where else? He riffles and hunts through dozens of envelope, ring-binder and box files. It's all work – research, old cuttings, various documents from years gone by, some browning with age. He presses the side of his head against the coolness of the walls to peek behind bookcases. He tilts his head at the floor looking for bumps, loose floor-boards. It's stripped-bare wood but there's a rug in the middle. He moves Colin's swivel chair to shift the rug away. He looks for extra joins in the floor-boards, places where a short section has been cut, but there aren't any. No floor cavity, no hidey-hole. But the obsession with the floor takes him now and he replaces the rug then paces carefully around the perimeter of Colin's den, as far as obstacles will allow, step by tiny step, listening and feeling with his feet for loose floor-boards. After a while of spiralling towards the centre and catching himself in a mirror at the head of a one-man, slow-motion conga, he thinks, *What the fuck am I doing?* He completes the spiral still. There's nothing. As far as he can tell, the office is clean.

He shuts the door behind him and heads downstairs to the cellar. A dim light bulb dangles on a flex. The manoeuvrable spaces beneath the house are cool, cramped and cobwebbed, smelling musty. There's nothing down here but junk. He can see that at a glance. He peeks with a torch in the obvious crannies and finds nothing but dirt and spiders. He claps his hands, swiping off the dust, and goes back upstairs.

Where else is there to check? Col would hardly hide something from Amy in the kitchen, dining room or living room. Unless he was being really devious, which was never him. He takes a look around the rest of the ground floor anyway, scanning more books and CDs and DVDs, going through the contents of the storage spaces, feeling awkward when he encounters things that are Amy's, feeling awkward raking through both their lives. It isn't right. He can see now that this is ill-conceived. He feels like a burglar. Perhaps a burglar would do a more thorough job. He shines his pocket Maglite behind any heavy furniture set against the walls. Nothing. No drugs, no magazines, no mysterious packages or envelopes. Clean.

He's been at it nearly ninety minutes now. He heads upstairs.

The toilet and the bathroom present no opportunity for concealment of anything. The bath is tile-panelled down the side, nothing removable. The cabinets are screwed to the wall. You couldn't slide anything behind them and hope to retrieve it without substantial DIY. There are no accessible floor cavities.

He proceeds to the guest bedroom, fully carpeted, he notes, ruling out the floorboards as a hiding place. A bed and little other furniture. A couple of bookcases, which he checks behind. The contents are – well, more books. Reference books, map books. What's he supposed to be looking for? There's a wardrobe with clothes, a mixture of Colin's and Amy's, hanging from the rail and nothing else but a broken lamp and an old manual typewriter on the floor. A built-in cupboard houses stacks of video cassettes. They're all labelled and innocent-looking. Sport, movies, documentaries, old TV series.

He enters the master bedroom – their bedroom, Amy and Col's. The sheets are mussed on one side from where she slept last night. He looks around, searching quickly – sock drawer, wardrobe, under the bed. Not that he's expecting to find anything anymore. He's just going through the motions now, eager to get out of there. In his haste, he pulls open Amy's underwear drawer and the sight of her panties reminds of him of the absurdity of what he's doing. Colin would've had to be the ultimate bluffer to hide anything in there. Still, Max gazes at the panties, twisted heaps of them, his thoughts burrowing in among them.

When he snaps out of it, he shuts the drawer, walks back out to the landing and closes the bedroom door behind him as though a wild animal is on the other side. He stands there for a moment, his hand still clasped around the door knob behind his back, suddenly wishing that Karen were here.

At least he's finished. There's nowhere left to look and he hasn't found anything.

Then his eyes rise to the loft-hatch in the ceiling.

8

When he hears her key in the lock he's sitting upright at the kitchen table. He doesn't rise when she comes in. He feels dirty when she looks at him from the doorway. He hopes he hasn't left any signs that he's been rummaging through their property, even though she knows that's precisely what he's been doing.

The oddness of the situation presses down on them both.

'Well,' says Amy. Max isn't sure if that's a question. He opens his mouth to speak and she gestures a halt. 'No. Don't say anything. Just – it's done, that's all. Now I can rest easy.' She gives him an inquiring look. 'I can, can't I?'

'Yes, of course,' he says, standing up and hitching his belt. 'Listen, if it's OK then, I'll shoot off. Got things to do, people to see. What about you? D'you need a lift anywhere?'

'No, no, I'm fine. Thanks, Max. I owe you a few drinks before you go back. I will see you, won't I?'

'Yeah, sure. I'm gonna be around for a while. Spending some time with the folks but visiting other people here and there. And in the meantime, if you need anything, call me.'

'I will.'

He steps forward and she stretches up on tiptoes to kiss his cheek, placing her hand unselfconsciously at the small of his back to balance herself. She feels the corner of something hard underneath his jacket and tries not to recoil. She lets the hand linger naturally until the brief embrace is over and she can draw it away casually, hoping he hasn't noticed, and she's following him down the hall to the front door.

''Bye, Max. And thanks again.'

'I mean it. Call me if you need anything.'

She stands on the doorstep and watches him walk to the kerb and start the car and pull out into the street, no last wave she notices, and she keeps watching until he's turned the corner at the end and disappeared from sight, and until a long time after that.

Max turns off Amy's street onto the main road then takes the third next turning on the left into a residential side street and finds a space to stop the car. He unfastens his seat belt, reaches behind him and pulls out the video cassette that's stuffed down the back of his waistband.

It's in an anonymous, black, plastic case. No insert, the cover, if there ever was one, removed. The label on the cassette inside has been scratched and torn off incompletely, some scraps of paper still adhering, but all identification gone.

He doesn't know what's on it. Amy had a VCR but he didn't want to risk watching it there in case she returned unexpectedly. It might be something to do with work. It might be perfectly innocent. But why was it hidden in the loft?

Whatever it is, it's best kept secret from Amy for now.

Except that she already knows about it.

Damn. Idiot. He should've nipped out and stashed it in the car before she got back. She tried not to show it, but he knew she could feel it there beneath his jacket when they embraced goodbye. He felt the pressure of the case against his ribs when her hand touched it. And however much she believes that she doesn't want to know, she will ask him about it, eventually. She's his sister-in-law: he knows what she's like.

The best thing he could do right now would be to get rid of it. Throw it in the river or rip out the tape, destroy it before he knows what's on it, before either of them do.

He studies it for a few moments more, to no conclusion, simply letting his imagination run riot, then puts the cassette back in its box and shoves it into the glove compartment before restarting the engine.

9

She negotiates the rest of Saturday all right, sort of.

After Max has gone she makes herself another cup of coffee on autopilot. She doesn't know why she's doing it, she was in the caff for two hours, she'll be peeing all afternoon. Nothing worse than coffee for that, she realises – the term 'diuretic' has become common currency – but she detests tea; always has; it's just as bad for you anyway, or good, depending on which newspaper you read or which company has commissioned the latest research. She'd be surprised if her parents, avid tea-drinkers both, had coffee in the house at all before whatever age they admitted that she had formed a liking for it. She wonders how old she was when she started drinking coffee. At what age did she start to become she, stamping the demands of her own personality on the world?

Well she certainly knows how to stamp them now. She feels bad about abandoning the wake yesterday. She's thinking particularly of Kat and Barbara and Roger, fellow teachers from her school, who probably used up a day's leave to attend for her sake, and she left them on their own in a room full of strangers miles away from anywhere. She'll have to face them on Monday morning. She knows they'll understand.

But she doesn't. Understand. She looks for her reflection in the kitchen window and it still isn't there. Not dark enough yet. She knows now. She knew all along, she was just trying to distract herself from it. She knows why she's making coffee.

The thing under Max's jacket. The thing he was hiding from her.

She thinks back to the way he stiffened as she kissed his cheek. Just a farewell, see-you-later kiss between normal, civilised adults. Little more than a peck. He flinched not because of the kiss but because he knew that she'd felt the thing under his jacket.

It was something hard. She felt a hard edge to it, a corner. It must've been something about the size of a book. If it was a book, probably a hardback. It could've been a video cassette, or possibly a DVD, though it seemed to stick out too much, unless it was more than one. A stack of DVDs. Or a package. A box or tin of some sort – containing what? Cocaine? Cannabis? Love letters?

OK, cut this out.

The mental self-command brings her up short. Max's Americanisms are rubbing off on her already. Poor Max. She can't dump this on him. He's lost someone, a brother, too. She needs to go easy. She made a deal with him. She didn't want to know and he wouldn't tell her. She has to put it out of her mind, think about something else.

She must phone her parents. She remembers, now, dozing and dreaming through the ringing of the phone this morning. That will've been them, even though they know not to call her before midday at the weekend. Of course, Max will've told them where she was when he went back yesterday, but she must phone them all the same. They'll be concerned. She has to reassure them – reassure Dad.

She gets her mother first, harping on about her returning to 'the London house', as if it weren't Amy's only property, as if she had a portfolio of them to choose from.

'Yes, I'm sorry, Mum, I should've let you know before I left yesterday.'

'But your things are still here. There's a suitcase full and more.'

'Yes, Mum, I'm sorry. I should've asked Max to bring them over.'

'You mean you should have picked them up before you went storming off back to London.'

'I wasn't storming anywhere, Mother. I just couldn't deal with it, all right? I don't have your stiff upper lip.'

'I do wish you'd stayed, though,' she goes on. 'David Cameron came to pay his respects.'

'Yes, I know. Max told me about it.'

'You mean you've spoken to Max since?'

'Yes, Mother.'

She never uses 'Mum' in these kinds of conversation. It stops her mother going down that route of inquiry; she doesn't want to let on to her that she hasn't just spoken to Max since but seen him face to face – not because she fears her mother's stricture but because she considers it none of her business.

'He was awfully disappointed not to meet you,' her

51

mother says, returning to the topic of Cameron.

'I'm sure he'll get over it.'

'Are you OK? That's the main thing. In that house on your own.'

'Mum, I can't just not live here. It's where I live, where I work.'

'I know, of course. But don't feel obliged to move back in so soon if you're not up to it. You know there's always a bed for you here, and the commute isn't impossible.'

'I know, and I'm grateful, really. But the sooner I get used to it the better. I need to—' She catches herself slipping into another Americanism and goes with it, too tired to produce a dignified alternative. 'I need to get my life back on track.'

'Whatever do you mean, dear? You haven't gone off the rails, have you?'

'No, I – I'm not expressing myself very well, am I?'

'You're still in shock. It takes a long time to get over losing a husband, and the funeral can just be another jolt to the system.'

She speaks as though from experience; the vicarious experience of friends, Amy supposes. They're both getting on a bit, her and Dad. That'll be the next thing.

'Am I in shock though, or am I in denial?'

'Nonsense,' snips her mother down the phone. 'No such thing. In denial of what? A lot of silly, psychiatric gobbledygook.'

'Maybe you're right.'

'I'll let your father speak to you. See if he can't make you talk sense.'

'Mum.'

She catches her before she hands the phone over to her father.

'Yes?'

'Thank you.'

She doesn't know whether she's thanking her for the offer of a home from home or for the support she's given her over the last two difficult weeks or for not upbraiding her even more than she has done for abandoning the wake yesterday. It's all she can say to her, the words of reluctant, daughterly love muffled and trapped in her aching throat – but her mother will know. She's still her mother.

'I'll put your father on, dear,' she says dispassionately.

Somewhere inside, she will know.

'Amy?'

'Dad?'

'You all right, love?'

'I'm fine, Dad, really.'

'I thought you might be. You're a strong lass. What's your mother been saying to you?'

'Oh, just fretting in her customary manner. Dad, I don't want to come home right now. There are some things I have to deal with on my own. Do you understand?'

'What kind of things? If it's anything we can help with—'

'Dad. They're – things I need to deal with on my own. I need to face work, I need to catch up at work, I need to build some new sense of normality. I need to be here. At least for now.'

'You know, need is a strong word. It takes a lot of justification.'

'I *have* to deal with on my own. Is that better?'

'I'm not trying to be pedantic, darling.'

'I know, Dad, I know. I'm sorry, I didn't mean to be petulant.'

'You only sounded it. I know you aren't.'

'Oh Dad . . . '

She tries to disguise an unexpected sob and it comes out as something between a sigh and a moan.

'Listen,' he says into the pause, 'whatever you want to do is fine. But don't forget us. We're here for you whenever you need us.'

'I'll be fine, Dad,' she says, becoming aware of how many times she's said that same word, 'Dad', over and over, the ultimate familiar, emotional kinship term in any patriarchal society, whatever language you translate it into. A primitive talisman she still clings to, even after ten years of marriage to Colin.

When the phone call is over, her thoughts start returning to the thing. She responds quickly to distract herself from it by going out to do some food shopping. There's nothing in the cupboards but tins and bottles and cereal cartons and jars of herbs and packets of spices that Colin once used for a recipe she'll never cook.

So she just pops down to the local supermarket on the High Street, trying to feel normal, ordinary. Pop, she thinks has to be the most common word in the English language; it can even mean father.When she walks along the brightly lit aisles, she finds herself actually looking at things consciously, thinking about them on some level. She's focusing, or at least as much as anyone normally does on a trip to the supermarket. Focusing on the items on the shelves. That's good. That's what you're supposed to do. That's ordinary. That's normal. Just focus.

She realises she's focusing too much. It's beginning to look like unwarranted scrutiny. She doesn't want to attract attention, the mad woman staring at a tin of baked beans. She moves on swiftly, almost forgetting bread in her haste, and having to go back for it and lose her place in the queue. She remembers wine.

Good – the checkout person is a girl she doesn't know. The Saturday staff change here a lot. She's glad it isn't someone who likes to chat a bit, who might remember her as a regular and ask where she's been recently, or even have heard the news and say something about being sorry for her loss.

That's what she fears. This is where her life is right now. Every encounter fraught with the possibility of tension and awkwardness. And not just with people. With things.

She makes the short walk back to the house carrying two bags of shopping without passing anyone she knows. She hasn't seen any of the neighbours yet, there's still that to face. They're friendly, sociable, but not too close – in that suburban London way; some will come knocking on the door when they realise she's back. In their own time. But eventually.

She puts away the shopping. She has to look after herself, she thinks, gazing with quiet satisfaction into the fridge, newly stocked with fish, meat, salads and vegetables. She mustn't let herself get run down. What now? Make another coffee? No, definitely not.

She finds herself strolling into Colin's den. It looks no different from how she left it. For a second she wonders if Max really touched anything at all. She glances about, unable to stop herself from imagining where the thing might've been hidden.

She mustn't do this.

If you want to know, ask him.

No, she mustn't do that either.

She pulls open the desk drawer. The cigarettes are gone. Her mind flashes back to his jacket in desperation, but that wasn't cigarettes. So he did search here, though. He must've thought they were Colin's.

She returns to the kitchen and pulls the pack she just bought out of the bottom of the shopping bag. As she lights one up she turns and faces the window.

Still too light – the late spring days too long.

10

She wakes up on the sofa in front of the television, her head propped like a broken doll's against the cushion. Mercifully, she hasn't put a crick in her neck. The TV is on but nothing is happening, or rather it's the same thing happening over and over again. It's what woke her eventually when she became aware of its wovenness into the fabric of her dreams: the same snatch of music repeated ad infinitum. When she opened her eyes and her vision unclouded, the DVD menu from before the film started was on the screen. The disc can't have finished that long ago, the screensaver hasn't kicked in yet.

One hand reaches over the edge of the sofa to the floor, scrabbling for the remote, and bumps against the ashtray. She shifts and peers over. Two stubs: acceptable. She peers out of the window before looking at the clock. It's still daylight out there. It will be till about eight or nine. What time is it now? Nearing seven. Christ, two hours she's been asleep. That isn't like her during the day. She's learned from her yoga teacher how and why stress can induce drowsiness. Now she won't get off again until the small hours.

She lights another cigarette, thinking that the day had time that needed killing anyway. She looks out of the window again at the enduring light, and thinks that it still does.

She wants to call him and she mustn't. That's what she was thinking when she fell asleep and that's what she's still thinking now. She fell asleep to damp her awareness of that persistent thought. She has to do something to distract herself or she knows she'll weaken and pick up the phone, and she can't, she won't, allow that to happen.

She rouses herself from the sofa and puts her shoes and jacket on. She has to get out of the house, if only for a walk. She deliberately leaves her mobile on the kitchen surface, recharging. When she's ready she locks the door behind her and heads the opposite way from usual down the street, walking away from the main road.

She crouches slightly, feeling ridiculous, as she scurries past the Taylors' house and the Binghams', hoping none of them will look out and catch sight of her. It feels like something out of a bad drama on the box, but she can't face them now. She'll make it up to them later – for her inability to acknowledge their concern for her, for the social inconvenience of her husband's death.

She can't remember the last time she left the house and didn't turn left. If she isn't in the car she's walking to the shops or the bus stop or the Tube station – all out the front garden and left. Even in the car they'd have been going left, towards the junction with the nearest and most useful main road.

She remembers what's down this way. Of course you do. The local topography is something you explore as soon as you move into a place, if not before, something you begin to familiarise yourself with straight away. But it's so long since she's been this way that the features reveal themselves as if out of a dream, the original reality transformed by the workings of an organic memory and her intervening experiences.

She knows there are other streets ahead just like theirs (*hers*, she mentally corrects herself), then, farther on, a footpath through a park and a bridge over a railway line. When she reaches the park she turns off and skirts it, unsure about going in at this late hour, though it's still light enough. Instead, she keeps to the path near to streets and houses. The presence of people and activity – even if it's just a group of boys loafing, or a car doing a three-point turn out of a cul-de-sac – makes her feel safe, connected to the world. It would be too easy right now to fade out of it altogether.

She gazes through the railings into the park, across it. Terraces of large houses stand on the opposite side, some whitewashed, reflecting evening sunlight. The trees in the park between the houses and her are glowing emerald and throwing long, solid shadows. The noise of traffic is just a drone far away, occasionally overlaid with the whine of a plane descending towards Heathrow; then the hiss and clatter of a train shooting along the track that marks the far boundary of the park, and sluicing under the footbridge.

Some lads are playing a game of football. Their cheers and shouts bounce off the walls of the houses behind her. A few late picnickers are still sitting on the grass, braving the last of the day. Lone strollers are following their dogs from tree to tree with plastic bags at the ready. None of these people resemble a discernible threat. On the contrary, they present an idyllic scene: the waning of a glorious spring day in a leafy corner of North London. It's everything she thought she wanted to get back to after that moment in the car in France: the fox incident – and how it somehow led her to thinking about the familiar world of good friends and dinner parties.

Recalling it now, a needle of nostalgia pushes through her, as it did then. She is here, now, back where she wanted to be in that moment, in the world she knows and cherishes, and all she wants now is to be back there in the car with Colin. That comforting world she longed to return to, she now finds, is empty.

If she goes into the park she's afraid something will happen to her. It isn't the people; it's the park itself, the open space; it intimidates her, beckoning and repelling.

She walks on until she's past the end of the park and on a street with more houses. She makes a point of not looking at her watch. She guesses she's been out of the house for half an hour, maybe forty minutes. She walks on for a further ten minutes, the streets turning into roads, less residential, more commercial.

She knows she's coming to the dual carriageway. She passes a pub she's never been in, then a car showroom and finally a petrol station at the junction at the end. There's nothing to walk along the dual carriageway for except PC World, a drive-in Burger King and an unreachable bus stop that no one ever uses and to which no bus ever comes, so she turns around and doubles back.

After ten minutes she's back at the park. She continues walking along its boundary, ignoring the open gates, past the point where she first joined it and on in the opposite direction.

Through the railings at this end she can see the pond, and restless ducks flapping in preparation to roost. Then some kids lobbing a basketball through a hoop. More youths, teenage boys and girls, rock on the swings in the play park, passing fags, swigging from cider tins, screaming and laughing at one another, too full of themselves, too full of young life, to look her way, no threat to anyone but themselves. At the end of the park she walks on for another ten minutes and eventually comes to a main road, not the High Street, a tributary of it. She turns the corner and is pulled up short by the pub standing in front of her.

The Oak Leaf. She'd forgotten. Colin and she went through a phase of going there every weekend for Sunday lunch. Nearly every Sunday, if they had nothing else on, for – what? A year, two years? It hasn't changed on the outside. But she'd forgotten, it was so long ago, seven years or more, and she's suddenly appalled at herself.

How could she forget the Oak Leaf? They used to come to it a different way, along the High Street. She never quite located it in her head at the end of the route she's taken tonight. The memories come rising up – the lazy pint, the sausage and mash, the Sunday crossword on the table between them – and she turns away. It's too much. She doesn't want to see that place. She can't bear those memories. It's too soon.

She knows the limits of her little world now. She can go no farther.

She looks at her watch and it's later than she thought, sneaking towards eight-fifteen already. The light in the sky has dimmed noticeably. She heads back towards the park and the turn-off for home.

The people in the park are thinning out now. The footballs and Frisbees are being stowed away. The last and hardiest of the picnickers are clearing up their litter and donning sweaters and jackets against the chill of the approaching night after a day spent in the warm sun.

At the gate, she pauses, feeling silly not to go in. She's here now, and it isn't dark yet. She steps in. For a moment she hovers just inside the boundary, mentally mapping the landscape, the locations of objects, bodies, barriers. Then she walks on, leaving the footpath and plodding across the grass right to the middle of the widest open space, where she stops.

This is the place. Here, as far from trees, buildings, people, as she can get. She revolves slowly, trying to take it all in – the fading light, the whisper of city noise, the warmth of the day leaking, bleeding away. The sun is out of sight, gone behind the rooftops and dipped below the horizon by now. The sky is a velvety blue, deepening towards the east. The first star catches the corner of her eye with an elusive twinkle. When she looks at it, it's gone, then a few seconds later she pins it. There's a second over there, and a third. As she gazes up at the sky, she's conscious of it as a dome cupped over her in the middle of this vast space, a dome whose radius feels delimited by the reach of her senses, when it could be expanded by her capacity to wonder.

But she knows that limit. She reached it up there on the bridge above the gorge. She left the experiencing, the wondering, to Colin.

So many stars are visible now that they're making her dizzy. She feels her consciousness weakening. She realise with some surprise that she's still turning around and around in circles. The wheeling sky is like the super-heightened reality of a dream fizzling away and leaving only the disappointment of wakefulness behind in its place.

How long has she been spinning? She shakily stops herself. What's she doing? She feels ill suddenly, like she did in front of the Oak Leaf – ill with a nostalgia, a yearning that can never be appeased.

After a while a train goes by with its windows lit up, and she registers how gloomy it's become, and that she's been standing staring like this for she doesn't know how long.

Do they lock the gates at night? She can see they're still open, and starts walking at a steady, unhurried pace, forcing back the dizzy, physical urge to veer from her course. If anyone comes to lock the gates they'll see her.

Before she reaches them, a noise stops her in her tracks. She turns around, peering towards a distant stand of trees. There it is again. A yap. The same sound rips across the park two, three more times. A fox. She keeps looking over at the trees, straining her eyes towards them. As if she'll see anything! It won't come out if it knows there are still people around. Reluctantly she turns away and heads for home, her ears still pricking for the bark of the fox behind the sound of her footsteps clipping through the streets.

When she gets in, she locks and bolts the front door behind her, hangs up her jacket and goes into the kitchen. She switches on the light and checks the time by the kitchen clock. Ten to nine.

It's dark out now. She turns instinctively to look at the window, but her reflection – it's still not there. She goes across and reaches towards the pane, and her ghostly hand appears in the glass.

That's strange: the window's open. She doesn't

60

remember having opened it at all today. She pulls it to and locks it, and when she pulls back her arm from the task she is there, Amy Trent, finally visible. A face stalking middle age – an appealing face, she's always happy to believe, but one which now finds itself draped over a musculature barely able and unwilling to smile. It's the face of a woman who is sad but also safe inside her little, lonely world.

She remembers she hasn't eaten, but isn't really bothered, doesn't even feel guilty about all that fresh food in the fridge asking to be cooked. Instead she grabs a bottle of red wine from the work surface then moves into the front room and switches on the TV.

When the screen comes to life, the same DVD menu is on it. The film she slept through this afternoon. The one where the Chicago moll calls her boyfriend 'sweetie'. He bought it for her last Christmas. She settles back with a glass of wine and selects PLAY.

She's sure she didn't open that window today. It must've been Colin – she means Max. She keeps doing that, and every time she forgets that he's gone it hurts a little less. Surely that must be a good thing, mustn't it? For a second though, reminded of Max, her mind goes back to the thing – until she sips her wine and lights a cigarette.

Think about the thing tomorrow, or hopefully not.

She sinks back into the sofa and focuses on the film, willing it to take her to another place, another time. Somewhere not here, not now.

11

'All right, come on, settle down,' Amy says spiritedly.

Her teacher-wants-your-attention voice cuts through the classroom hubbub and the kids shuffle in their seats to face her. Year Twelve, the first year of 'A'-level English Lit. Only nine of them this year, a smaller group than last. A nice group. Here out of choice, even if their attention strays from time to time. Something happens to them when they make the decision to carry on once the compulsory stage of school, up to the age of sixteen, is over. They become – interested; and it makes them interesting. Not like the kids in the lower forms, who are just a drain on her energy most of the time. It always makes her wonder how they turn into the same kids sitting here now, looking reasonably engaged.

'All right,' she says again, unable to escape the all-purpose phrase she long ago substituted for 'OK' when she got bored and self-conscious of that. She has their attention anchored now.

'Homework: common everyday phrases coined by Shakespeare. Be honest, who's done it?'

Nearly everyone puts a hand in the air. The one or two who don't keep their heads down.

'Ooh. I'm impressed. So come on then, what did you find?'

She fixes Laura, a white girl at one of the middle-row desks. A middling student who'll probably get a C, though Amy's sure, as she is of them all, that she could get an A if she worked just that bit harder. She wonders if their choice of desks reflects any kind of pecking order, or whether it's simply that the shirkers gravitate to the back. Sometimes she thinks she can see patterns: it's how the mind works. Some teachers stick to surnames, even with the 'A'-level students. That's how the mind works too, though she hates the impersonalness of it herself.

'Yes, Laura.'

'A heart of gold, Miss.'

The girl speaks with the strident, Jamaican/Estuary, back vowels that all the kids use nowadays. It sounds gobby and confrontational to Amy's generation, a fact she knows from how other teachers moan about it in the staff room, but she's sure it isn't meant that way. They use it to each other as well, friends and enemies alike. The swaggering tone of voice no longer signifies a challenge or a threat, not in today's London. If it's backed up with action, yes; otherwise Amy has trained herself to overlook it.

'Very good, Laura. Any idea which play that comes from?'

'Is it *Henry V*, Miss?'

'It is indeed. All right. Any others? James.'

She points at a plump boy sitting near the back.

'Pitched battle, Miss.'

'Very good, James. And the play?'

'*Taming of the Shrew*.'

'Good grief, well done. Have you read *The Taming of the Shrew*?'

'No, Miss.'

She didn't think he would've done, it isn't one of this year's set texts and she knows it wasn't on last year's GCSE syllabus either, but she lives in constant hope that some of them might devote at least a modicum of their time to some wider reading.

'All right. Others? Steven.'

'Steve, Miss.'

'Sor-ry.' She makes a meal of the apology as she always does and the kids laugh on cue. 'Steve.'

'It's all Greek to me.'

'Very good. And is it really all Greek to you or are you getting the hang of it now?'

'Pretty much so, Miss.'

'Pretty much what? All Greek or getting the hang of it?'

'Both.'

'Even French is all Greek to Steve,' says one of the other class jokers, and everyone has a good laugh.

'All right,' says Amy, 'so tell me. Did you all get this from the same website?'

Another round of laughter. She thinks of the weekend she spent (today is the Tuesday of her second week back) poring over her *Collected Works* and various Shakespeare biographies, tracking down the references the old-fashioned way, while the kids printed a list off a screen. She doesn't feel aggrieved; actually she feels satisfied. It helped her to fill the weekend. For most of it she managed to dodge the cold, comfortless grip of self-pity.

'Let's hear some more then.'

'Laughing stock, Miss,' one of them calls out. 'From *Merry Wives of Windsor*.'

'Knock, knock. Who's there?' says another.

'No,' says Amy. 'Really?'

'It's on the list, Miss. From *Macbeth*.'

'I never realised that. I thought it was some old music hall joke.'

'See, even you learn something new every day.'

'That's not one of Shakespeare's too, is it?' she says, and there's more laughter. She's got them warmed up now.

'A sorry sight, Miss.'

This is Winston, who sits near the front but rarely speaks unprompted. He's clever, imaginative – she knows he is from his essays – a hard worker, but reticent. Whenever she nudges him into saying something, he usually tries to bring it round to his favourite subject: 'It's like in music . . .' is a frequent gambit of his.

This isn't like him: maybe he wants her attention, maybe he's bored of waiting to be asked. But he hasn't put his hand up. That's not like him. Something in him now as she turns and looks him in the eye restrains her from responding. She waits, knowing there's more.

Afterwards it will be as if she'd known what was coming.

'The truth will out. The naked truth. What's done is done. Dead as a doornail. Good riddance. To thine own self be true.'

Amy is stunned into silence. She goes cold at first. Then the burning starts. It begins at the edges of her ears and radiates through her face to the tip of her nose. Her shoulders tingle, then her arms, her thighs....

The class is silent. She doesn't know whether it's because they've understood the awful subtext or because they're all too busy looking at how stunned she is. She can't speak. The silence holds, lengthens. No one can speak.

Winston's eyes hold hers. They're not guarded, nor are they proud. She should feel anger, she can sense its potency brewing inside her, wanting to erupt, but when she looks into his eyes there isn't anything to be angry at. She's just stunned, in shock, flushing, blood and adrenaline gushing uselessly through her system.

She has to control it. Like she would've failed to do on the bridge. Like Colin was able to; imagine she's Colin.

'Yes,' she says at last, swallowing drily on the word. She stares down at her notes on the desk, but it's all swimming before her eyes. 'Yes. Those are all from Shakespeare. So many – circumstances, situations, emotions that we'd find it hard to express without him.'

'We'd find other ways though, Miss.'

It's Winston again. She can't look at him. She feels weak. She *has* to look at him.

I'm the teacher, I'm in charge.

She raises her eyes to his. His gaze is still locked on hers, steady, frank, perhaps a little mournful, even, with teenage wisdom.

What does he want from her?

'Go on.'

'I mean we'd find other ways to express ourselves without Shakespeare. If he'd never lived there'd be others. Other writers 'n' poets 'n' stuff. Or off the TV or the internet . . . '

She finds she isn't listening anymore. It's a skill that's gone, vapourised in the shock. She relinquishes his gaze and picks up her copy of the play they're studying and opens it at the bookmark, holding it up between the class and herself, aware that she's using it as an emotional crutch – in fact, a shield. Aware that *they* know that.

'OK, everyone, page thirty-seven, please. This speech of Iago's. I want an analysis of the rhyme scheme and the imagery, so heads down and let's get to work. Separate sheet of paper, name at the top.' She forces herself to be teacherly, it's like putting on a mask or a suit of armour, but she's aware that she said 'OK'. She reverted to a previous teacher-self, weaker, less formed, and clutching at the old talismans.

A hand goes up gingerly at the back.

'How many words, Miss?'

The question bugs her. Annoyance flares out of the shock like a firework through fog.

'Just get on with it! I'm going out for a few minutes but I want it finished and handed in by the end of the class. Is that clear?'

A murmur around the room – a teacher going out and leaving them on their own, a thing rarely heard of – as they bend over their desks.

'I'll be back in a few minutes.'

She goes out the door, trying not to hurry. She pulls it to carefully behind her. Then she scurries along the corridor to the ladies' staff toilet.

There's no one inside. She locks herself in a cubicle and pukes into the toilet bowl. Only the once. A quickly ejected dollop of it – the sandwich she had for lunch. She dry-heaves afterwards but nothing else comes up. She pulls down the lid and sits on it, wiping her wet eyes, nose and mouth with horrible institution bog-roll. When she's finished, she lifts up the lid between her legs and tosses it into the bowl then flushes it all away.

She remains sitting where she is. The tears in her eyes now aren't vomit tears but real ones again. She tries to stop them, tries to pull herself together, but she can't. Why would he say those things? It wasn't coincidence, she could tell by the look in his eyes, he wanted to make a point. It was as if he'd planned it. But why? What does Winston have against her? What's she done to him? Why was it so personal?

It makes no sense. Since she's been back at work, the other teachers have all expressed their sympathy and support, but none of the pupils has mentioned the loss of her husband. She suspects that while she was away they were warned not to by the headmaster. He'll have regarded that as the sensitive option. So why this? Why now? She doesn't know why she's crying even. It isn't clear that it was meant to hurt her. But it did. The sudden upset stunned her and the effort not to show it made her freeze.

She controls the tears, wipes them on her cuff, sniffs, clears her head. Maybe it meant something else; but the message she read into it, which probably the whole class read into it, was callous in its execution if not in its intent. Was that its intent? To be cruel for cruelty's sake? She recalls his eyes. No; there was something in them trying to make a connection, some level of empathy – she's certain of it.

Outside the cubicle, she washes her face, takes a drink of water from the cold tap and dries herself with paper towels. She looks in the mirror. They'll see she's been crying but she can't help that. At least they won't know she puked. She has to get back. Thank God the writing task should keep them busy until the bell goes.

Outside the classroom door she can hear discussion within but not the words or particular voices. When she opens it, the talk ceases. By the time she's stepped inside, all heads are down, including Winston's. Saying nothing, she sits at her desk and spends the longest thirty minutes of her life looking at the same page without reading it.

At the end of the period, she barely raises her head as they stand up and start to shuffle out. She doesn't look at Winston. She knows she should. She should confront him now, not leave it, or it could go on. Instead, she waits until he's out the door then asks one of the other boys, Steve, to stay behind for a minute. He's a bright boy and always seems genuine with her.

'Steve,' she says when the others are gone, 'you know Winston, don't you?'

'Yeah, course I do, Miss.'

'I mean d'you know him well? Is he a friend?'

'I know him a bit. You know.'

'I just wondered if he doesn't like me for some reason. Not that I'm asking anyone to like me but—'

This isn't going well. She's handling it all wrong. Is this how that other, former teacher-self would handle it? By procrastinating, then blundering in too late? Playing the 'me' card? To the wrong player?

'I dunno, Miss.'

'I'm sorry, Steve,' she says trying to pull it back, 'I'm not asking you to rat on anyone. Or am I? I'm sorry if it seems I am.'

'Maybe you should ask him, Miss.'

That stops her bumbling. She's about to tell him, yes, of course, he's absolutely right, when he continues.

'Look, what he said before was proper out of order. He shouldn't've said that. I'm sorry, Miss. I'm sorry about your husband. Mr Denby told us not to say anything but—'

She's cried already. She's all right now. She's OK with

this.

'It's OK, Steve. It's all right. Thank you.'

He hitches up his bag and walks to the door. Before going out he turns and looks back at her over his shoulder.

'Everyone's sorry, Miss. Including Winston.'

12

In the staff room, later, she feels that she's pulled herself sufficiently together and is calm enough to talk to Roger about it. He's been as nice as pie to her since she's been back, despite her having abandoned him in the wilds of Berkshire after the funeral.

She speaks softly over his shoulder while he sits leafing through a science magazine, asking him his impressions of Winston.

'Winston Paige?' he says, turning from an article on quantum mechanics to look at her over the tops of his glasses. 'What's he been up to?'

'I don't want to go into details, Rodge. He said something inappropriate in class.'

'Inappropriate? Paige? He's not usually a back-talker.'

'Well it wasn't back-talk exactly.'

'So what was it?'

Amy glances about; she doesn't want everyone to hear. She moves around him so they're properly face to face.

'It was a comment about Colin – my husband Colin. At least I think it was.'

Roger's head lowers toward the magazine but he's no longer looking at it.

'If it was inappropriate we should go to Denby with it. That sort of behaviour can't be allowed. He'll get himself suspended if he's not careful.'

'No, I don't want it to go to Denby. I'm not even sure if it was meant to be offensive. He could've meant something else, something inoffensive. I don't know. I just wondered if you knew much about him. I know you don't teach him anymore but—'

'He was never much good at science, I know that. Good with computers, but they all are nowadays.'

'I mean anything about his background, his home life.'

'I've met his parents at PTAs. They seemed – normal, I guess. They came last year. You were there.'

'Before I taught him, though. Didn't speak to them, wouldn't know who they were.'

'Look, if you want to ask anyone you should be asking Roz. She's probably the one who knows him best out of the lot of us.'

Roz is a music teacher. Lincoln. Roz Lincoln. Amy isn't close with her, not out of any dislike, simply that she's one of a newer staff intake and hangs out with the teachers of her own generation. Amy's only common ground with Roz Lincoln is the staff room, where they're friendly and civil without having to think very much about who the other person is.

'He's always talking about music.'

'Yes. Keyboards, isn't it?' says Roger. 'You haven't seen him play in the school jazz band?'

'No, I—'

She lets the unformed thought die away, conscious of her lack of interest in extra-curricular events, and knowing there's no need to account for herself to Roger.

'He's not bad. Gets a lot of individual tuition from Roz, I believe. If anyone knows anything about him, she probably will. I mean, they must talk about something other than music sometimes, mustn't they?'

She thanks him and makes a mental note to speak with Roz Lincoln.

Later, when she's around.

After she thinks of what she's going to say to her.

Maybe.

13

It's late, that's all. She doesn't know how late.

Something woke her, drove her to get out of bed. Now she's at the bedroom window with the edge of the curtain drawn back, peeking out into the back garden. It's very dark out there, little residual light from the street on this side of the house at night. She waits, peering out, letting her eyes find the little light there is. She doesn't know if it's science but it's something she knows instinctively: no matter how dark you think it is, there's always some light, no matter how little, even in deep space. You can't keep light out any more than you can keep it in.

Still she isn't sure, she can't make herself certain, whether she saw a movement out there in the dark.

She leaves the window and moves through the house, going downstairs to the dining room without turning a light on. She stands at the French windows, gazing out.

There's something out there; she's sure of it now.

She concentrates, willing new depths of light to emerge from the dark. A shape forms from the light her eyes have drunk in and moves forward to within ten feet of where she is standing on the other side of the glass.

A fox. A young one, by the look of it. Male or female, she has no idea. She can't see in this lack of light. Not that she knows what to look for anyway. It looks smallish, not fully grown, and healthy looking – sleek, compact – as far as she can tell.

She opens her eyes wider and the creature becomes more visible; it isn't just a trick of the mind. She realises she's holding her breath. She lets it out slowly and draws it in again patiently, finding a measured, tranquil rhythm.

Just stay still and watch.

For minutes she stands like this, breathing in, breathing out, controlling her breath as if its presence might otherwise be detected by the fox. The fox also remains motionless; maybe it can see her through the glass. It's checking her out or at least satisfying itself that there's no further movement where a moment ago it thinks it saw some. It doesn't back away, it doesn't advance. It holds its ground, as if the ground has value.

What might it want? What do all foxes want? A mate? Too young.

Food.

Apart from whatever other living creatures might be around on the ground in the middle of the night (she thinks of mice and hedgehogs, though hedgehogs are said to be disappearing and it's years since she last saw one, even in her parents' garden where she saw them often as a child) the only food source is the bin on the other side of the house and the only way there for it is around – or through.

She continues watching, not wondering what it will do, just watching; and all it does is watch back. She doesn't know how much time passes. No time. All time. Just watching each other.

Then the fox flinches, crooks a foreleg back suddenly at a noise that only it has heard. The ears prick up higher, pointier than they were already, if that is possible – if her ability to perceive and understand that subtle adjustment of the sense organs is possible in such meagre light; it freezes like a statue, but only for a split second before it turns to the side and points its snout towards the spout of the kitchen drain. It moves three, four paces, confident at last that there is no threat.

She watches it range around the patio, relaxed now, exploring.

Amy is aware of this wonderful opportunity. As she follows it around the yard as it snuffles at this and that interesting scent, ears and tail signalling awareness of its surroundings and its exact place in the world, she tries to immerse herself – her *self* – in the natural world, the world of the fox. A world free of emotion; but also a world free of rationality and logic. You can pin those anthropomorphisms onto it like a granny shawl onto a wolf but you can't ignore the fact that it lives purely on instinct and a will to survive. Even that isn't right: she can't help adding the last anthropomorphism herself. Not a will to survive. The will, like emotions and logic, is just the illusive and nonsensical product of another cold, hungry dream in the natural world of the fox, in the world of all but humans. It lives simply on an instinct to survive. In fact, to be.

After a while it returns to the window, stands looking at it again, looking, it seems, at her. Then an extraordinary thing happens. It moves close and rears up on its hind legs, its front paws propping it up against the French window.

She hears its claws ticking on the edge of the glass. It's as if it's reaching towards her, gesturing something. It's like it's her it wants, though that cannot be. Perhaps it's asking her for passage through the house to get at the bins in the street out front. This is such a ridiculous notion that she almost laughs, but she's too captivated by what it will do next. Should she open the door for it, she wonders. Whoever heard of such a thing – letting a fox into the house? If she let it in it could do anything: shit on the floor and then head straight for the kitchen. So why does she trust it not to?

If she opened the front door first and made sure it had a clear passage, it wouldn't feel trapped. It would sense its escape route and go that way.

She tiptoes through the house and unlocks and unchains it, trying to turn the key and slide the bolt without noise, aware of the late hour, the neighbours, the cautious animal outside. Then she returns quietly to the French windows at the back of the house, ready to open them.

The fox has gone.

She isn't gutted or surprised but her heart sinks a little. She wonders why she feels disappointed. She's been questioning her emotions in this way a lot recently, for obvious reasons. What is she feeling? Why? These are the questions she's been asking herself, and they're becoming monotonous.

And what does the fox have to do with any of it?

At some point, looking out of the window, waiting for the creature to return, she must've decided to go to bed because that's where she finds herself waking up the next morning. She knows it wasn't a dream, but for some as yet unfathomable reason at the back of her heart she's reluctant to accept that conclusion too soon.

She flips the duvet back and, breaking a lifetime's habit, jumps out of bed the moment she's awake, to check the front door. She can't remember shutting it – if she ever opened it to let the fox through.

To her relief, the door is both closed and locked, proving nothing.

14

In the next class with Winston, Amy tries to behave as if nothing has happened and, to her relief, he and the rest of the group follow her lead. It's another example to her of how fast they mature once they've stuck with their education by choice – and theirs, not someone else's.

At the end of the double period, ninety minutes on the character of Desdemona and all its significations, she plucks up her courage and asks Winston to stay behind for a word. She shuts the classroom door behind the last student to depart then turns to face the wordless void separating her and this boy before her.

Winston's eyes flicker at her, a deep, searching brown, but intermittently hooding themselves, dipping to the immaculate toecaps of his Asics trainers then back to her; straight into her eyes for long seconds on end: *What?*

She waits. She doesn't want to jump in, gums flapping wildly. That will achieve nothing, not for her, not for him. She lets the silence sustain between them. But the more he looks at her, the more her eyes and nose swell, making her feel that her face is betraying her emotions – emotions beyond her control.

Still, she lets the silence hold, and manages to dam the threatening tears. Winston is spending more and more of the time looking at his trainers, occasionally casting her meaningful looks that she doesn't know how to interpret. In the meantime, he ignores it when her brow knits into a question. But it doesn't matter. Her worst fear has come to pass. She cannot speak. She remembers a dozen questions stacked up in her mind for just this moment, for just this person, yet none will pass her lips.

'You all right, Miss?'

It almost makes her jump. She doesn't expect him to be the first to speak, despite her own speechlessness.

'Yes, I—' Words end. The wordless void resumes. She fights through it, induces the birth of speech. 'What was that the other day?'

'What, Miss?'

'Oh come on, Winston, you're worth more than that.' She's struggling towards the right words and making a fool of herself along the way with non sequiturs. 'Don't cheapen yourself.' She's riding high on words plucked from nowhere. Or maybe from the commonest discourse of a tabloid-TV nation. By that realisation, her confidence is pricked and deflated. It's like riding a space-hopper and kicking it with spurs. She needs Colin around to remind her not to say and do these things.

'I don't know what you mean, Miss.'

'That . . . tirade you came out with. That stuff from Shakespeare.'

'It's what you asked us to do for homework, Miss.'

'But—'

'What d'you mean, tirade?'

He has her on the back foot again. She shuts down and holds up her hands in a gesture she's never used before. Something she's picked up from Max or Winston maybe, she doesn't know which. Not just a signal of desperation; a locking down of channels, a talk-to-the-hand.

'I'm sorry,' she says. 'You'd better get along to your next class.'

'I've got a free period now, innit, Miss?'

'Right. Well, whatever. Just go, please.'

'I'm not a bad guy, Miss, you know what I mean?'

'Yes, Winston,' she says mechanically.

'And I'm sorry about your husband and all.'

He's being nice now. Is that what this is all about? He upsetting her as a prelude to coming on all nice? Soft-soaping? Angling for a way into her good books? It throws some perspective on his motivation, though she isn't sure what. There's something behind it, she's sure of that. *Even if it's only a schoolboy crush*, she thinks as he slopes out, to an old Average White Band tune running in her head.

15

That night, she dreams about the fox again. Or is it real? This isn't a question in retrospect but one she asks herself as it's happening. Is she really rising from bed and tiptoeing downstairs to peer through the French windows? Or is she lying in bed dreaming she's doing it? Her inability to distinguish between the two states alarms her, because it feels like a failure of the real world, not the dream world. But this is something she can obsess about on the Tube for five minutes in the morning. Right now she has a needy fox to attend.

She knows tonight from the way it paws at the glass like before that it wants to get into the house, and probably through it to the bins out the front. She knows it with the force of a conviction. She reaches up and turns the key in the lock that opens the French windows, but stops herself from opening them. She recalls the other night, and goes to unlock and open the front door in readiness.

This time, when she returns, the fox is still there. She opens the French windows, using slow movements. As the doors part, the fox skips back, but only a pace, cautious but curious. She watches its handsome, pointed face inspecting the new space that has just appeared to it.

There is a long moment of waiting and stillness. The fox deliberates, second-guessing the possibilities of danger. Tentatively it pushes a paw forward into the unknown territory, its head flicking back, its eyes looking straight into hers, seeking permission, approval, reassurance. There she goes again, imposing human interpretations on the creature's actions, but that's how she apprehends them.

For a moment Amy doesn't know what to do. It almost turns into a moment of panic. She doesn't want to do anything that will scare the animal away but she can't think how to make it trust her. She takes a long, deep, steady, yogic breath, holds it and steps one pace back away from the fox's entrance, only releasing the breath slowly and noiselessly across the stretch of a full minute. She hasn't been to classes for a while but she can still time it with that internal clock whose measurements she hasn't lost the skill to read.

She watches without moving as the fox slinks through the doors, muzzle pointed straight ahead towards its purpose, and whips through the dining room, claws skittering on the hard, varnished floorboards, into the passage way and out through the front door, down the path and onto the street.

Without so much as a by your leave.

It's a crass thought but, as she locks up, it sends Amy back to bed distracted and happy, until she falls back asleep.

Only with the advancing light of morning does the dream that had initially awoken her in the night come to memory. It's a dream of Winston, chanting his refrain: *'The truth will out, the naked truth, what's done is done, dead as a doornail, good riddance, to thine own self be true.'*

Even before she opens her eyes, while her mind is still swimming below the surface of sleep, her dream-self replays the dream-memory over and over – *'The truth will out, the naked truth . . .'* – and when she awakes, the words cross over with her.

16

Max tries. For a whole week, he tries.

First he tries to destroy the tape. No, the tape isn't indestructible, just his curiosity about what's on it. As much as he shouldn't, he wants to know.

He tells himself it isn't prurient. He tells himself there may be nothing lewd or incriminating at all on it, that it could be just an old movie that he forgot to return to Blockbusters – and that happened to be stashed away in an envelope in the loft for an obscure but innocent reason that will forever remain beyond fathoming.

And if it's something else? Then he tells himself that he has a duty to know, because Amy, if she ever does ask him, has a right to know, and destroying the tape without knowing, without being able to tell her, will be denying her that right forever. So he can't destroy it. That's shifting the blame from himself, but it's one decision made.

The next is to watch it, and he tries to do that too.

He tries to watch it at his parents' house but whenever he's staying over, they're always around, sitting up to the most ridiculous hours, one, two in the morning, enjoying the freedom from the clock of the retired, and wanting to spend all the time they can with the son they see so little of, and who's the only son they have now, and who's still staying up so they are too. It's always one or the other of them, sometimes both. When they do concede and go up before him it's such a business to hook up the arcane VHS player, which has been disconnected in favour of a DVD player and a subscription to Sky, and then figure out how to work the various remotes, that the task by that time of night seems hopelessly beyond contemplation. He loves his parents but there are reasons why he can't be there for long.

He tries again in a four-star hotel in Nottingham while visiting a friend whose cramped bedsit stretches to a bit less floor space than he's happy with. The hotel room has satellite provision and a DVD player, but no VCR. His own mild surprise tells him maybe he's been in Tunisia too long. Undaunted, he goes to the trouble of phoning room service and asking if they can provide one, to which they politely respond as if he's just requested to send a telegram.

Finally, while staying in some friends' house in Cambridge, he finds a video-recorder hooked up to an ancient but still-working portable colour telly teetering on a stack of files in a tiny office under the stairs. There's no cause to dissemble, he simply has to ask and he has the office to himself.

Feeding the tape into the machine, he agonises one last time over how much he really wants to do this. As long as he keeps the tape then he protects Amy's right to know what's on it. It doesn't mean he has to watch it. But there's his right involved too – his right to know who his brother was, whatever he was. And besides, this is Colin. How bad can it be? However bad, it might help him understand: understand something, anything. Even if it's something about himself.

He sits back and watches the screen light up. It looks like some kind of film coming up. Company logos, production credits, obviously done on the cheap. Then the title, nothing fancy, plain, block lettering across the screen, CCTV SEX, along with the explanation that it's 100% FROM REAL CCTV CAMERA FOOTAGE.

The premise of the film requires no further introduction, but the makers have gone to the trouble of giving each scenario an onscreen title. CHANGING ROOM QUICKIE is first up, footage of a couple screwing in a department store changing room, unaware of the camera, which may or may not be concealed, bringing questions of privacy and legality to mind; the girl has her ass on a little bench with her skirt up around her ribs, while her boyfriend quivers between her legs with his trousers down around his knees, positioned awkwardly, semi-crouching, semi-kneeling. The image is monochrome and grainy, and the camera filming from such a distance that little of any titillation can be seen. The clip goes on for three and a half minutes, nothing changing, the guy's backside, half-hidden by his skewed shirt-tail, moving in and out between the girl's legs. You can barely see her face. In the absence of recorded sound, the makers have added some bad hip hop music, and by bad Max means terrible.

The second scenario is titled BLOWING HORN IN THE CAR PARK and consists of one badly framed shot of a woman apparently giving a man a blow job in the front seat of a car.

What dim lighting there is shows the top of a blonde head bobbing into and out of view through the front windscreen, while the guy's face stays hidden in shadow. After two minutes of this, Max thinks he's got the message. He presses the STOP button and ejects the tape without bothering to fast forward or rewind it.

OK, so now he knows: it was porn all along. Which isn't so bad. It isn't what Amy will want to hear, but it could've been something worse. It could've been a murder confession, home movie footage of Colin romping at a gay orgy, or any of the other wild, dark fantasies that have been rampaging in his head for the last seven days.

But something doesn't make sense, a couple of things actually. If Colin was into pornography, then why didn't he find anymore in the house? Maybe he'd had a purge, thrown it all out. But if so, why not this? Why was this still hidden in the loft? Maybe he'd forgotten it was there. But why was it put there in the first place? If there was other stuff, why wasn't that in the loft? And if he'd cleared the other stuff out of the loft, then why did he keep this? Of all things, why did he keep this? It isn't even good porn. Nobody is going to get a thrill out of this.

There has to be something special about it, possibly something important.

Resigning himself to ploughing through the rest, he pushes the tape back in and presses picture fast forward to the next grim scenario.

Not knowing whether he will find anything or nothing.

17

Dreams continue to punctuate Amy's sleep throughout the nights that follow. Dreams about Colin, often involving dangerous wildlife and frantic chases through exotic scenery, jostle against dreams of Winston and his words. Notably, the dreams about Colin are dreams of action while those about Winston are the opposite – hardly dreams at all even, for they contain nothing resembling a narrative. There's only the sound of the words in Winston's voice, pulsing through her brain with feverish obsession. She isn't even sure if there's a face or even a mouth. Even Beckett gave his voices a mouth. It's as though her dream-self has reduced Winston's physical presence to nothing till there's only his voice, because what is a voice but vibrations in the air, and supposing those vibrations slacken with time but never stop completely, in the way that light never stops completely, might they not be audible, albeit at an ever-diminishing level, forever? Shakespeare's spoken words travelling eternally through time. Perhaps there's some ironic comfort to be taken from that thought.

If she isn't sure whether this is a dream or not, she's more certain that the fox wasn't a dream but a reality. The morning after she thought she'd let it through the house, there were mud traces where its paws must've trodden it in from the garden. She'd become convinced it had really happened by then, in any case, and she can think of no other explanation for the mud being where it was.

In the intervening days however the animal hasn't been back. She doesn't know that of course, hasn't been up all night, every night, waiting and watching, but because she hasn't been aroused from sleep, as she seemed to be before by its presence outside, she trusts it hasn't been back.

The days go on routinely enough. She goes to work, she teaches her classes, she gossips with her friends over lunch, she marks her students' assignments, she gets home by five, she watches *The Weakest Link*, she has a shower, she cooks for herself, she opens a bottle of wine, she reads a book or listens to music or watches more TV, then she goes to bed. These are the outward forms of her daily life.

With the inner forms, she's making progress in rebuilding them. She has put the cigarettes away, back in Colin's desk drawer, without having touched them for days. She can even confront Colin's name now without being impaled by a nauseous, curling sensation of anguish. The neighbours have paid their various visits and she's spoken to them calmly and tearlessly and perhaps even rationally, and they seemed to understand, or made successful imitations of doing so. She's making an effort to eat and drink her five portions of fruit and veg a day, and she's walking the two miles to work and back instead of taking the lazy bus or Tube option, and next weekend she'll look at the notices pinned up in the local supermarket and see if there isn't a new yoga class somewhere not too far away that she can join.

Whatever was on Winston's mind that time in the Shakespeare lesson must have passed because, while his behaviour and attitude in class hasn't exactly returned to normal since then, it has improved instead. He always paid attention, she could see that, but now he's participating more actively, speaking out, engaging with questions, chipping in to discussions, when before he would've stayed silent. He can be moody and touchy but he isn't brooding; she can see no sign that he's keeping anything inside, bottling something up. It's as if the 'Shakespeare incident', as she labels it in her mind, is forgotten by him, or meant nothing in the first place.

She continues to wonder what his motivation was, but she can dissociate the sting of that memory from the boy who interacts with her on a more relaxed footing now. In time she'll stop pondering it and perhaps believe that there really was no motive behind it at all, that it in fact it was said with no special intent, with no thought on his part to what she, of all people, who'd just lost her husband, might infer.

Except she knows that he's more intelligent and self-aware than that. This knowledge keeps her concern alive, but she can sense it mellowing with time and the distractions of other daily cares.

She thinks about having that conversation with Roz Lincoln, Winston's music teacher, but the longer things go along smoothly between him and her, the more she puts it off, until putting it off turns into not seeing much point in it anymore.

No, her relationship with Winston is OK, less a concern

and more an ache you barely notice anymore. Part of life's background; like Colin, now. Part of her background, her life's résumé. And that isn't meant to be cynical. She's glad, after a fashion – as glad as glad can be, for her.

But there's another part of this inner life of hers that she's trying to rebuild that isn't so resolutely upbeat. Namely, the thing.

She hasn't started to think of it with a capital 'T' yet, but it keeps creeping back into her thoughts so persistently that she's almost ready to bestow that level of bogeyman status upon it. The John Carpenter horror movie of the same name keeps coming back to mind, and H.P. Lovecraft, whose tales she read as a girl. *The Thing on the Doorstep*. The Thing Under Max's Jacket. Like Lovecraft's inter-dimensional demons, it's something from another world that ought not to have crossed over into this one; from Colin's private world, which she still can't work out whether it really existed or not, into hers; and if it did exist, and she just never saw it, then what is the thing?

Her mind keeps running riot with it. Sometimes it's like an explosion, a flashbulb tableau while she's sipping a coffee at work or sitting on the loo thinking of nothing in particular. She'll have stabbing visions of Colin screwing another woman, screwing two other women at the same time, or snorting coke off some tart's lap in a toilet in the back of a bar in the City while she's at home cooking dinner and wondering when he's going to get back from the long, hard day those slave drivers put him through. At other times it's a ruminative vision that sneaks up on her unawares and lingers, entrancing her imagination. It's like lifting and marvelling at the underside of a rotting log crawling with lice and worms, while her real earth-body stands staring at the kitchen window. At those times, when her mind draws her to those darker places, she's quite capable of constructing entire epic narratives of chronic unfaithfulness, serial womanising, addictive gambling, slavish pornography, debauched levels of drug and alcohol abuse, affairs with friends' young daughters, or even sons.

At those times, in those moments, she knows she's being stupid, that to have carried on such a lifestyle without her knowledge, Colin would've had to be in league with not just the devil but the Kray twins and Myra Hindley too, all of whom were last at liberty probably before he was born. She always reminds herself that this is Colin she's thinking about; she knows what his life was like, and this isn't it.

But then herself will come back, reminding her that Max was definitely hiding something down the back of his trousers. The thing under the jacket. It always comes back to the thing.

She resists contacting Max, though she said she will while he's still in England. She knows he's still here from phone conversations with her mother; she never thinks to question how her mother knows, because that doesn't seem important.

One thing she can take comfort from is that whatever the thing is, at least it's out of the house. She's reclaimed the freedom of her own home. This sense of having achieved some accommodation with her new life as a lone-person household leads Amy Trent on to her next decision.

It's time to go and see Colin.

18

She takes the overland train out to the nearest station then a booked taxi the rest of the way to Edward and Christine's village. She has no choice but public transport, since she asked Edward before the funeral to get rid of the car; at the time, any practical considerations aside, it was a sealed box of memories that she didn't trust and had no wish to keep or open. She disliked driving anyway and would never use it. She wonders if one day she'll regret getting him to sell it for her – all the money's doing is languishing in her bank account, another small chip for careless City greed-merchants to fool around with – but today isn't that day.

All along her route to Berkshire there are hassles and delays: it's a weekend, it's to be expected on public transport in and around London. But that's all something she can put up with, grumbling to no one but herself about it, without recrimination. At the end of the journey the sun is still out and, when she walks up the path to the front porch, the garden is in full bloom and Christine is able to greet her with a smile that carries if not good cheer, exactly, then at least a heartfelt welcome.

'I'm so glad you called,' Christine says, shepherding her inside. 'We've been looking after it – the grave.' She gives the word a stoically prosaic emphasis. 'Fresh flowers every day. Well, there's no need to tell you that. Of course we've been looking after it.' She leans in a little closer on Amy's arm. 'I just wanted you to know. We're going to look after him properly for you.'

'Oh Christine . . . '

'Just so that you can come anytime you like. Like today.'

'I know. I thought it was time. I felt ready. And thanks.'

'What's a good mother-in-law for? I know they make jokes about us but we're not all bad, you know.'

Amy smiles fondly. She's heard the line before but not for such a long time.

They settle in the front room with the smell of French polish, and it strikes Amy how long it is since she was last here. Her mind tags on the automatic rider *Not since Colin died*, but she queries that, trying to remember if she was brought here in that awful fortnight between the accident and the funeral. Her memories of that interlude are still as foggy as they ever were, or ever will be; of that she's sure, because that's the way she wants to keep them. It's time to build a new mental edifice of who her husband was. That's why she came here today – to lay the foundation stone. And she's already sounding pompous to herself. She'll have to check that. She isn't the world's only widow, nor the first.

Plenty deal, so deal.

'Max is here.'

'Is he?'

'Oh yes. Not gone back to Tunisia yet. Don't know what that girl of his is going to be thinking.'

Just as Amy is about to say 'So he told you about Karen?' she stops herself from falling into an old and familiar family trap.

'What girl's this?'

Christine sees through it, Amy can tell immediately, but she's gracious enough to play along.

'He thinks we don't know there's a certain someone in his life, but he never stops talking about her. It's so obvious.'

'Is Edward here?' Amy asks, hoping to change the subject.

The breeze in Christine's face drops.

'Oh, he's off at some horse race or other. Took the car out at the crack of dawn. Knew you were coming, sends his love.'

'That's nice.' It's a bland thing to say but she feels comfortable with it. She won't rise to Christine's evident disapproval of Edward's absence. Today requires stability above all, bland stability.

'Would you like a cup of tea?'

That's nice too – Christine's need for stability; the brew from a South Asian bush leaf providing her particular kind of ontological security.

'D'you have coffee?'

'Of course we have coffee, dear.'

As Christine departs to the kitchen, Amy remembers another thing she loves about her: she never needs to re-ask her how many sugars, or whether she takes milk. Even Amy's own mother still has to ask, always pretending she's checking the latest update, which is bull: she's always taken milk and one sugar, for as long as she can remember drinking coffee.

While Christine is making the hot drinks, Amy needs a wee after the journey out. She heads for the upstairs loo because she recalls the downstairs one having a noisy plumbing problem that sounds like the maiden voyage of the QE2. Stepping out of the toilet room after she's had her pee, she comes up short against Max. He emerges from the bathroom at the end of the hall, still a little wet, with dewdrops of shower water on his shoulders, and clad in a bath towel wrapped around his lower half, with his hair wet and lanky, and she realises with a mental start that he has a hairy chest. She can't work out why that surprises her at first. Her mind casts back for memories of when she might've seen it before – in a swimming pool or at the beach – until she realises they've never been on holiday together. So why does it take her aback? The answer comes to her in a sliver of thought-time: Colin's chest was smooth, and he never shaved it.

'Oh. Sorry,' she says automatically, bumbling out of his way as he heads to the bedroom.

Sorry for what? the back part of her mind kicks in. *For being here? For existing? For knowing about the thing under the jacket and making him feel uncomfortable?*

'Don't be silly,' he says, grinning a grin that at once disarms any further thoughts as barbed as the one she just had. He couldn't look any less uncomfortable.

'I thought you'd be staying with friends, or I'd've been in touch.'

She's speaking for speaking's sake to work through the sudden encounter with his semi-nakedness, while he stands there unselfconsciously.

'I came down last night.' Down – as if she should know where from. 'You going to see Colin's grave?' he says.

'Yes.' She looks away from him as she says it.

'We'll go together, all three of us. I shan't be long.'

Shan't. The time in England is eroding his Americanisms and replacing them with the old, comfortable forms of home.

'That's good,' she says, another soothing banality.

He disappears along the landing and into the guest bedroom.

Downstairs Christine has brought the tea and coffee through from the kitchen on a tray with a plate of biscuits; anything less would have constituted unacceptable presentation.

'So how are you coping, dear?'

'Oh, you know,' says Amy, knowing that Christine won't know, that Christine knows little or nothing of her life in London. 'Life goes on, as they say.'

'How's Stephen?'

Amy is slightly puzzled, then realises she means her father. She can't recall Christine ever referring to him by name before. It's always 'your father'.

'He's fine. I suppose, anyway. I haven't seen them for a while but they were fine on the phone last time we spoke.'

Amy realises she's talking about both her parents while Christine only asked her about her dad. It fractures her understanding of their exchange, and when she finds herself trying to imagine Christine asking 'How's Marian?' about her mother it strikes her how little common ground the two women have, Christine and her mother, not enough apparently even to simply rub along. If they can be said to have a relationship at all it's one of mutual politeness and sufferance for the convenience of others.

'I heard David Cameron showed up,' Amy says, to change the topic. 'At the – Did he speak to you?'

'Yes, of course, my love. He seemed sincere enough. Well, he was nice about it. Said all the right things. Looked as though he meant it. Didn't stay long. At least he didn't have cameras following him. When I first heard he was coming I was rather concerned it might turn into some awful PR event.'

'When did you first hear?'

'Only the day before. Edward had organised it all through a Rotary Club pal of his. It was his idea. It seemed appropriate enough since Colin was going to interview him anyway.'

'It was his friend's idea?' says Amy, puzzled.

'No, Edward's.'

'But – so Edward did it all, did he, on his own?'

A flicker of an odd emotion crosses Christine's face as she opens her mouth to speak. Is it puzzlement, irritation, embarrassment? Before Amy can pin it down, it evaporates with the entrance of Max, all clean and dressed.

'Ah, you're up at last then?' says Christine, her whole face altered to something approaching motherly brightness, that special blend of solicitousness and mischief.

'I've been up for hours working in bed on the laptop.'

'Chatting to that girl of yours, more like,' says Christine, targeting Amy with a discreet wink that detonates Amy's expectations of a moment ago, when Christine seemed about to voice some buried grievance. 'Skyping, they call it, apparently.'

'Shall we get going?' says Max. 'Then we can get some lunch in the pub afterwards. My treat.'

The weather's lovely now and the cemetery is only a couple of miles' walk but they take Max's car all the same. Some of the lanes can be muddy any time of year and there's no sense getting shoes and trousers dirty when Amy's brought nothing to change into for the journey home.

They park outside the church and tread down the slope of the church yard to Colin's grave without a word. At the edge of it they become silently awkward, over-conscious of one another's proximity, and spread themselves out around three sides of the plot. The headstone says COLIN TRENT, LOVING HUSBAND, BROTHER AND SON. It's nice, like Edward sending his love, and the tea, and the knowing about the milk and sugar.

She thought she came here today to say something to Colin. Not murmur into the ground like some mad person but say something to him in her heart. It didn't matter that she wasn't alone, that they weren't alone together. She'd be able to say it in her heart and hear it in her mind – whatever it was. Even if it was just telling him what she'd been doing without him, what had been happening in her life. But now that she's here she looks down at the grave, tiny sparse shoots of grass appearing in the soil, and can say nothing. It's as if Colin isn't there.

As they all crouch together to place fresh flowers, a screeching noise swoops overhead in the sky and Amy looks up from the ground to see a dazzling green flock of five – six – seven ring-necked parakeets.

19

Afterwards, Christine veers away on her own at the churchyard gate.

'Christine,' says Amy, 'the pub's this way.'

'Oh, listen, you two go and enjoy yourselves. I'll get some lunch back at home, I don't want to sit drinking all afternoon.'

'Mum, why don't you take the car?' says Max.

'Why? Are you going to drink too much?'

'No, not at all. We're just going to grab a bite and a pint. Sure you don't want to come?'

'Pub lunches can turn into bad habits.' Amy's mind flashes on The Oak Leaf. 'A brisk walk followed by a sandwich with a cup of tea will sort me out, thank you.'

Amy feels awkward again, being alone with Max. She doesn't want it to look as though she manouevred them together, or Christine out of the picture, not that there is any reason she knows of for anyone to think that. On the other hand, they did say that they'd go for a drink together. Just a little more notice would've been helpful; she wasn't expecting to find him here today.

Once they're sitting at a table next to the window though with a pint and a Bloody Mary in front of them and reading a menu she feels calmer.

'So, you're still here. I was worried I might've missed you, that you'd gone back already.'

'Worried?'

'We said we'd go for a drink. I haven't called you about it and I didn't want you to think I wasn't into it for some reason.'

'No. I should've been going back this weekend but I'm gonna stay a bit longer. It's a bad time for my parents right now and I – I wanna stick around for a bit. See they're all right.'

'How long for?'

'I dunno. Few more weeks. Just till things settle down for them.'

Amy senses he's holding something back but she lets it go.

'What about Karen?'

'She's coping. She understands. And anyway, she might come over if business slackens off a bit.'

'Oh, that'd be nice. I'd like to meet her. See what kind of woman got you to settle down.'

'Well that's the thing. Now that I'm settled I'm realising the world is full of responsibilities and I have to be big enough to take them on, and one of those is my parents. However well or badly I got on with them growing up, I have to take that on. I can see that now. I couldn't before. I was such a shit to them.'

'No you weren't. When?'

'When? Every time I failed to get in touch, let them know where I was or what I was doing. Every time I missed their birthdays. Every time I stayed away from them.'

'You've had your own life to lead. You've seen them when you can.'

'But not enough. I mean look at them. They're getting old. They *are* old. I missed the getting part. And now Colin's gone . . . '

'Shall we order something to eat. I'm starving.'

The menu is reasonable pub fare. Amy chooses a grilled tuna steak with buttered new potatoes and salad and Max orders the beer-battered haddock and chips with mushy peas. Max fetches Amy a large glass of white wine from the bar but keeps to his first pint, taking it steady for the car.

'Cheers,' says Amy chinking her wine against his still half-full pint, careful not to spill any. She moves it to her lips and the first sip is so sharp and clean, so cold and clear, that it stimulates her to just blurt it out.

'Max, I know you found something.' Max looks at her over his pint, frozen mid-tilt, getting the smell of beer without a touch of it. 'At the house.'

'I know,' he says after a while, lowering the glass without drinking.

'I know you know. I mean we both know. I just wanted – it to be out in the open.'

'Why?' says Max. There's annoyance in his voice. It's the first time she's heard him annoyed with her. She pauses, thrown out. 'You said you didn't want to know,' he says. 'You could've gone on pretending. That would've been easier for both of us.'

'So it's something serious.'

'No, that's not what I'm saying.'

'And I'm not saying that I want to know what it is. I just wanted it out in the open. I don't like pretending. I can't pretend. If I could pretend I'd be a bloody actor, not a schoolteacher.'

She feels herself rising to his annoyance, his mild anger, with a dose of her own.

'All right. All right. Anyway, it's nothing. It's innocuous. Nothing that besmirches his memory. OK?'

'Was it a video?'

'It—' He slumps his shoulders and hangs his head, deflated, at his wit's end.

'It felt like a video.'

'Yes, yes, it was a video.'

'OK. I just wanted to know. I thought it was a video. Have you watched it?' Max thinks about lying but it's too late. 'You just said it was innocuous. You must've seen it?'

'Yes,' he says. 'I have. And it is innocuous. This is starting to get silly, like that word "silly". Innocuous, innocuous, innocuous. OK? Now no more questions. It's gone. It was nothing and it's gone. Not worth remembering or thinking about.'

'H'm. Like that's gonna happen.'

'Which is why we shouldn't have gone here in the first place. You said you wouldn't.'

'I know. I'm sorry. It's not fair. I told you I was a bitch.' That raises a laugh out of him at least. 'But please just answer me one more question.'

'Oh, Amy . . . '

'Where did you find it?'

'Ooohh,' he moans, his face in his hands. 'I should not be getting into this.'

'Just tell me where it was. Please, Max. And then I'll stop bugging you.'

He looks her in the eye between hands pushing through his hair.

'It was in the loft.'

'The loft?' She thinks about this for a moment. 'The sneaky bastard.'

'That doesn't mean it was something he was hiding from you, you know? He cold've been hiding it from someone else.'

She nearly asks who, but the lack of a plausible answer is too obvious. Anyway, she's said enough, asked enough; more than she intended.

'I'm sorry, Max. I had to ask. I had to ask just that much.'

'I know. I know what you're like, you know? I haven't been so remote that I haven't been paying attention.'

The food arrives and they set to the work of negotiating their way through the rest of lunch without returning to the subject.

20

The fox comes back that night.

She wakes not at a noise but at a presence. It's the middle of the night, the streets and gardens either side of the house are empty and still, but she knows it's there.

She slips into her dressing gown and goes downstairs in the dark. She has a sense memory of everything in her path now, she's getting so used to the routine. She stands at the French windows for a few minutes, waiting for the animal to emerge out of the darkness of the garden, letting her eyes guzzle the thin light of the night sky.

And there it is.

Tentative, as usual: it's a fox, it never stops behaving as a fox. Even when it stands up and taps at the glass it seems to her a typically fox-like thing to do, done in a typically fox-like fashion. But again she forgot to open the front door for it to get out. She turns away from the window, away from the fox, to go and open it when she's stopped by a voice from the other side of the glass.

'Amy . . . '

She wakes up.

It's morning. The alarm still hasn't gone off – another ten minutes. She has to get up for school anyway. But she lies there enjoying the ten minutes' grace, not falling asleep again but thinking about the fox.

It wasn't a dream. Yes, maybe she dreamt about it afterwards and woke up at that startling moment when the fox spoke her name. But it really happened. She's sure of it. She can remember something the fox told her. Not everything, but they spoke together. She can't remember the details, can't quote the words. That part was like a dream, yes, it was like trying to catch smoke in your hand because her mind had trouble accepting a talking fox, which is an understandable thing for a human mind to do.

But she knows it wasn't a dream because of that one thing she remembers the fox telling her. She knows it was real because the fox told her who he is.

The fox is Colin.

21

Amy finds yoga classes near by but they're at a health club, one of a chain that's recently colonised the local high streets. Joining the classes means joining the club – but she can afford it, and it brings access to all the other classes and facilities. They have a pool there: she should take up swimming. It's near enough to school that she's able to squeeze in a Tuesday lunchtime yoga class and then there's a Thursday evening one that she can manage, and twice a week is quite enough for now. Both those classes are Ashtanga, a more active and dynamic form than the Hatha yoga she did before, but once she starts she finds that there are also moments of quiet and stillness in which she can let herself drift away, shedding the trappings of the mind.

She takes up practising meditation at home. She's reasonably supple, she can easily sit for an hour in a semi-lotus posture and not have any trouble standing up and walking away afterwards. At first she meditates to music. It helps her mind shut down. Light instrumental jazz usually does it. Later, she turns off the music and absorbs the silence of the house around her in the night, trying to go deeper, let her mind go free, let it all fall away, so that she can get back to the memory of the things that the fox said to her that night. Once her preconceptions are gone, the reality, however improbable, will be all that's left.

One Thursday after yoga class she runs into Winston in the foyer of the club; he's also just leaving. Not runs into, exactly. She's almost out the door when she hears him call out behind her.

'Miss. Miss Amy.'

She turns around and her solar plexus constricts, as it has a habit of doing at moments like these; a hot dump of adrenaline shoots through her insides.

'Hold up, Miss.'

He's out of school uniform, casually dressed, 'streety', but she recognises him under the cap. He's swinging a leather hold-all in one hand and clutching his phone in the other.

'I didn't know you came here,' she says.

'I come for the weights, Miss. What you here for? I definitely ain't seen you training the weights.'

'No. Yoga.'

'Is that like connecting with your inner self, all that kinda stuff? I'm interested in that kinda stuff.'

'Well, you should come along then. There's plenty of men do it. See if you like it.'

The words come out without thought. What's she saying? Does she really want one of her students joining her yoga class?

'I will do, Miss, but when I'm not busy with my weights I'm busy with other things. You know, the music. And homework and revision an' stuff, course.'

'Of course.'

They're hovering at the door. Somebody tries to come in and they both acknowledge that they're in the way and step aside.

'Listen, Miss, do you wanna come for a drink?'

'What? No, I—'

'Are you already going somewhere?'

'No. Just home.'

Immediately, but too late, she realises that's the wrong thing to say.

'Aw, come on then. Just one drink. I want to hear some more about yoga.' And then he says a funny thing. 'It'd be an honour, Miss.'

An honour. When did she last feel honoured? It's as good a reason as any now that she's over the shock of bumping into him. Maybe it's time she did something impulsive to break out of the routine for an hour.

'OK. But just one, all right?'

'Wicked.'

The evening is warm and they walk to the nearest pub along her homeward route that doesn't look too 'local' or rough. Nowhere with bouncers on the door. She should know the decent pubs round here. She begins to feel responsible, the oh-shit-I'm-the-teacher syndrome kicking in, which she realises is ridiculous under these circumstances.

'There's a nice pub at the next junction, Miss,' says Winston helpfully. 'It's a Wetherspoon's but it's quiet on a night and the prices are cheap, know what I mean?'

'OK, fine. Slow down a bit though.'

'Sorry, Miss. I'm well known for walkin' fast. I keep forgettin'.'

'So what's this music stuff? I didn't know about that.'

'Really, Miss? I thoght everyone knew.'

'You're in the – school jazz band or something?'

'Ho, you're breakin' my heart, Miss. Course I'm in the school jazz band. You never seen us play?'

'Sorry, afraid not.'

'Oh, we is wicked, man.'

'What do you play?'

'We play Mingus, we play Stanley Clarke—'

'I meant what do *you* play?'

'Oh. Keyboards, Miss. Piano, Rhodes, Fairlight, all that kinda stuff.'

'Wow. Sounds – impressive.'

'You don't know much about jazz, do you, Miss?'

'No.'

'That's cool. Maybe I can teach the teacher something. You can teach me about yoga and I can teach you about jazz.'

The pub, when they get there, is not her idea of quiet but they're able to grab a table off someone leaving, so she can't grumble. She insists on paying for her own drink but is happy to send Winston to the bar, after wondering if there can be anything wrong with this and working out whether the boy is eighteen and legal yet: he must be, he's about to take his A-levels. She's even less worried when he comes back with the red wine that she ordered and just a non-alcoholic drink for himself, a bottle of apple and mango J2O.

'You see, with jazz, it's about lettin' yourself go, an' that's where I see a comparison with yoga. What d'you reckon?'

'About what?'

'Is jazz like yoga, Miss? In yoga do you let yourself go? You know, like when you're concentrating or meditating.'

'I don't know. I can only imagine what it's like to be a jazz musician. Just as I can only imagine what it's like to be a poet.' Old habit makes her bring the subject round to literature, the teacher in her lurking beneath the skin. They're doing *The Waste Land* in the 'A'-level class. 'When Eliot was writing, do you think he let himself go?' she asks.

'Ah, I know what you're tryin' to imply because Eliot is more free-form than your traditional poets like Shelley or Wordsworth or any a those guys.'

'Am I?'

'But Eliot's not as free-form as he looks 'cos of all the allusions that he puts in. It's all studied, man. It's all carefully controlled. So I don't see him as lettin' himself go like that.'

'Why not? We assume, and we have pretty good evidence, that Eliot was a well-read man. If he had all those allusions up here already' – she tapped the side of her head with a finger – 'just waiting to come out at the flow of his pen, couldn't he lose himself in the writing? Let himself go, as you put it.'

'Yeah, but when you're playing and it's a great solo or it's right in the groove you find a stillness. You reach a place where you can really let go without having to think at all.'

An image flashes through her mind of Colin standing on the bungee platform, completely still, centred, ready to leap. She works past it.

'Eliot wrote about the "still centre", remember?' she says. 'Sounds like you two have a lot in common. But it also seems to me that with music – and language – you're still constrained by the demands or limits of a system.'

'I'm not talking about the system though. I'm not talking about finding the right analogy or hitting the right notes in the right way. If you know the system inside out, if you've studied and practised at it for years an' years, then it's second nature, you don't have to think about it anymore. I'm talking about being taken to a special place through actually hearing it and knowing it's you doing it. And it is a still place. It's contentment. It's bliss. Or at least it is when it all goes right on the night.'

'Do you play in other bands?'

'Yeah, I play in a crew called Jazzocracy. It's kind of a cross between jazz and hip hop. You know, the way Ronny Jordan took it, back in the Nineties.'

'Erm, no, I've no i— Ronny – ?'

'Jordan, Miss. Jazz guitarist. You never heard "So What?"?'

A memory of a lesson from Colin draws her away to a mental perusal of his CD collection, still on the shelves at home.

'Isn't that Miles Davis?'

'Aah, so you do know something about jazz. Ronny Jordan an' DJ Krush produced the definitive version. It's got a backbeat . . . ' Winston's lips go into some sort of spasm that produces the most amazing sound, and his fists play an imaginary kit of drums. 'An' then Ronny's guitar comes in . . . Ne-nun ne-nun ne-nun nun, now nun, ne-nun ne-nun ne-nun nun-nun, now nun – '

Amy finds herself singing along.

'Yeah, I know that tune,' she says excitedly.

'From *A Kind of Blue*, right?'

'No. I mean, yes, but I know the version you're singing. It's faster than the original, isn't it? And the melody's played on a guitar instead of a trumpet.'

'Well, it's Paul Chambers playin' it on the bass on the original, but yeah, that's it. That's the Ronny Jordan version. It is brilliant. I seen him do it live once. They totally extemporised it, man. Truly wicked. That's the kinda vibe we're aiming for with Jazzocracy.'

'I'd love to see you live,' she hears herself saying.

'I'd love to play for you,' he says.

She hurries on past the implication of intimacy between them.

'You've got me all excited about jazz now, I'll listen to it with new ears.'

'It's such a wide open field that it's difficult to think where to start. You just gotta get stuck in an' see what you like an' then follow the connections. This guy played with this other guy so maybe his album's gonna be worth checkin' out as well. Know what I mean? That sort a thing. An' you've got to follow your instincts.'

She isn't sure what he means by that last bit but thinks she's taken in enough about jazz for the first lesson. She's learnt who Ronny Jordan is, that's plenty for now. She has to say something though.

'You – must have a massive CD collection.'

Hardly a million miles from the same subject.

'I got a few but I never listen to CDs anymore. Mostly I'm on YouTube and Spotify. They're good places to find new acts that you've never come across before or read about once in some magazine years ago.'

Now she's lost. What is Spotify? Fortunately it's his turn to pick a topic.

'So tell us about yoga, Miss. What's special about it?'

'Winston, you don't have to keep calling me "Miss".
We're outside school hours. We're just two civilians, all right?'

'Sorry. It's a hard habit to break.'

'Well, what do you want to know about yoga? Surely
everybody's got their own idea of what it's about.'

'I've got my own idea about what chemistry's about but
that doesn't mean anything, not even to me.'

'So why should my idea of yoga mean anything more?'
She isn't fishing for compliments – really.

'Cos you like yoga an' I hate chemistry.'

'Ah, right. Logic. I wasn't ready for that.'

'What, you don't think I can think logically?'

'No, I didn't mean that and you know it,' she says giving
him an arch smack on the wrist.

'I can have you up on charges for that, Miss' he says, and
she's pleased with herself when she recognises he's joking.

'Yoga's – not a skill or talent. Not like what you do, or
what T.S. Eliot does, for that matter. It's all natural. There's
nothing to learn beforehand, no second nature. It's first nature.
The only thing you have to learn is to breathe.'

'What, you mean like that joke about David Beckham
wearing earphones to tell him to breathe in 'n' breathe out?'

'Oh, that's years old, that. You have to do something
called ujaya breathing, keeping it under control. By focusing on
your breathing you relinquish other thoughts. Then once you've
mastered the breathing you can lose yourself. Not lose yourself
exactly. It's actually about finding your . . . ' She's searching for
the right word, *le mot just*. Calmness, centre? But these are trite
notions that they've already gone beyond.

'Your real self,' says Winston.

'Yes. Your real self. Your pure self.'

She hopes he's getting it. She doesn't know quite what
she's trying to say, suddenly it sounds like talk for the sake of
talk. A part of her wants to get away now, perhaps the wine is
going to her head a little and the situation of being here chatting
with Winston in a pub is just confusing things. It's been fun but
that's enough. She's opened up all she wants to. She's back at the
moment where she doesn't know what to say next and wonders
whether it's a conversation she wants to keep going.

'Is music your life?' she asks him, for want of a more

sparkling gambit.

'Do you mean have I got a partner? Am I going out with someone?'

He cuts straight through to a subtext she didn't see coming round the corner. While one part of her blanches, another part thinks, *Damn, he's good.*

'I'm sorry. That's none of my business. I shouldn't be asking.' She's overplaying it now, or that's how she imagines he might see it.

'Nah, it's a fair question. But like I said, I'm too busy with my music an' school work an' stuff. There'll be plenty a time for that later.'

'Bullshit,' she says without thinking. 'Excuse me, but you're an eighteen-year-old boy. Of course you're thinking about sex.'

'Beggin' your pardon, Miss, but I didn't say I wasn't, or that I wasn't gettin' any. I'm just sayin' there's no one special right now.'

She's sorry she asked. Terms like 'plenty of time for *that*' (her mental italics) and 'getting any' aren't exactly her cup of tea. She decides to try a new conversational tack, and before she knows it she's steamed right in with what's really on her mind.

'Do you believe in . . . well, the paranormal? The supernatural. Ghosts. That kind of thing.' She means talking animals, but can't bring herself to say it: visions of Eddie Murphy in *Doctor Dolittle.*

'You is joking, right?' Immediately she senses some barrier going up. 'Has someone put you up to this?' He throws back a manly swig of his J2O, acting suddenly aggrieved.

'What?' She's genuinely puzzled. She's clearly said something terribly wrong here.

'The hoodoo voodoo stuff. What they say about me around school.'

'I don't know what they say about you. Really, Winston. I'm sorry, I—'

'Is this about that thing I said to you in class that time?'

'What—' Now she's doubly blindsided.

'That Shakespeare stuff.'

She holds back to let him go on speaking but he's

offering her a way in.

'You chose some very specific quotes that could've been misconstrued at a time when I'd just lost my husband.'

Winston's head is hanging.

'I know, Miss,' he says. 'I'm truly sorry. I shouldn't't've said anything. I shoulda kept my mouth shut, as usual. I know the others know more than me, leastways in English Lit they do. That's why I never used to say nothin' in class 'cos sometimes you just gotta listen an' learn, innit? Even if it's from the other students. So that used to shut me up.' Then he looks up at her. 'But it never meant they was any better than me, 'cos they might know it all, but most of 'em have never been in the zone.'

Amy gives him a puzzled look. The zone?

'I mean losin' yourself in music,' he explains. 'That was mine, man. They could keep their Shakespeare as long as I had the music. Then you asked us to find them quotes an' it was somethin' I could understand for once, a task I could get my head round. But I never planned it for 'em to come out the way they did. That's the thing. I didn't choose them, it was more like they chose me.'

'You mean you didn't know what you were saying?'

'I dunno. I know that once they were out it felt right, it felt like they needed sayin', an' I couldn't take 'em back anyway. Shit, man, I can explain jazz but I can't explain this. It was like I was meant to tell you somethin', maybe somethin' I didn't really understand myself. I didn't mean to upset you though.'

'Then what did you mean to do?'

'It felt more like a prediction.'

'Felt?'

'Listen, Miss, it doesn't matter.'

'What do you mean, felt?'

''S like I said, I can't explain it.'

Amy puts up a barrier now with her silence.

'Look,' he continues, 'maybe we should be callin' it a night. My folks're gonna be thinkin' I've run away from home again. An' that's a joke by the way, a'ight?'

'A'ight,' she says, attempting a levity that falls flat.

'I'm glad I ran into you tonight, Miss. It was good to have a talk an' that, know what I mean? Clear the air a bit.'

'Yeah,' says Amy Trent, weighing it all up and feeling

short-changed. 'I'll see you tomorrow.'

He's getting up. She feels like she's blown something and that the only way to set it right is to explain why she asked him about ghosts and the supernatural, seeing that that's what seemed to upset him, but she can't tell him about the fox. Can she?

'I can walk you home if you like or get you a cab or something,' he says, perhaps a little guiltily.

'No, I'm fine. It's not far. I was going to be walking anyway. I'll see you tomorrow. And if you ever feel like a chat at school it's all right by me. About Eliot – and stuff.'

She'll leave the fox thing for now. She isn't ready to appear mad just yet.

But she wants to know more.

She wants to know how they make coffee granules. She wants to know that her reflection will be there in the kitchen window when she looks for it. She wants to know what Colin said to her when he visited her in the night as a fox. She wants to know what Christine was about to say that morning when Max walked into the room. She wants to know what's on the tape that Max found in her loft. And after tonight she still wants to know why Winston said what he did in the Shakespeare class.

What did he mean by a prediction?

When she gets home she writes down the words as she remembers them, trying to focus on her memory of the event itself and filter out the dream of Winston's voice. She looks at what she's written, satisfied that it's accurately remembered.

The truth will out. The naked truth. What's done is done. Dead as a doornail. Good riddance. To thine own self be true.

She's been over it enough times in her mind to recognise that this is what he said, but she never looked at it written down before, and it helps her to break it down in her mind.

The truth will out, the naked truth. What truth? The truth about her? That a part of her feels guilty about the circumstances of the accident? That she's a coward who didn't want to do the jump? The truth about Colin? Something connected with what's on the tape? But how could Winston know about any of that?

What's done is done. What? It must be some deed, some act, but what? And again by whom? Herself? Colin? Some betrayal? Despite her having tried to conjure some scarlet woman of the imagination at the funeral, she doesn't really believe that sexual betrayal was something Colin ever did. She'd have seen signs of it and, unless the tape proves otherwise, she knows it wasn't in his nature. She's also sure thousands of betrayed women have thought this before her, and that only makes her doubly sure. Something in the past – that's all she can get from the phrase.

Dead as a doornail. Well that part's obvious.

Good riddance. That's the cruel part, the part she can't forgive or forget. If it was meant about Colin then why? What did Colin ever do to Winston? Maybe, though, it's meant to be her saying it. A prediction? One day will she think this about Colin? After discovering some awful truth about him? She's letting her mind run away now. She has to bring herself back to the Colin she's sure she knows. But even up there on the bridge there was a part of him she admitted she would never know. What if it's in that unknown part that the seed of the prediction originates?

Then the last part. *To thine own self be true.* That seems to be addressed directly to her. It sounds positive, the proverbial silver lining, but meaning what? They talked about the self tonight in the context of jazz and yoga. Is this connected?

Shit. If she can't imagine a plausible theory by which to understand all this then why was she so wound up by it in the first place? But she was. Not wound up: shaken up. She still can't shake off the feeling that it was intended to mean something. But if Winston can't explain what he'd meant by it – and she can think of no reason to disbelieve him – then how can she ever find out?

And another thing, seemingly separate: what did he mean tonight by his comment about hoodoo voodoo? If nothing else, this brings her to a decision. She'll talk to Roz Lincoln, Winston's music teacher, listen to what she has to say about him. She'll do it tomorrow.

22

The next morning Amy happens to be leaving the house at the same time as Trish Taylor from next door and they chat as they walk to the junction together.

'You've heard about the fox?' Trish says at one point.

Amy tunes in to the topic with caution. What does her neighbour know about it?

'What fox?'

'There's been one in the gardens. Haven't you seen it? I've seen it in your garden.'

'What about it?'

'It's had somebody's cat. That woman at number thirty-four, who's just had that loft extension built.'

'Rubbish,' says Amy. 'Foxes don't kill cats. I've never heard of it anyway.'

'I'm only telling you what I've heard. I was a bit sceptical myself, to be honest, but what else could've done it? It was found in a right state, by all accounts.' Exactly whose accounts, Amy wonders. 'If it wasn't a fox it must've been a dog. She was talking about getting someone in, though.'

'Getting who in?'

'Some kind of pest control. For foxes. That's what she was talking about anyway. Apparently there's some company that does it at night. But get this – with a gun. Now normally I wouldn't get involved but do you want some stranger creeping around the streets at night with a loaded gun? I certainly don't, fox or no fox.'

Amy is thinking that she mustn't let it through the house again. She must keep it in the enclosure of the back gardens where it's safe, away from the streets and this madman who will be on the loose. But of course it will always find a way through or around. That's its nature. Whatever it is, it's still a fox.

'You must tell her,' she says to Trish.

'Tell who what?'

'The woman at number thirty-four. Tell her how you feel about it.'

'Well . . . I will if she goes ahead with it. Like I said, it was only talk.'

'Well we've got to stop her. Start a petition or something.'

'I'm not sure about that. I'm a bit busy. I've got a job and a family to run.'

Amy stops herself from going on.

'Yes, of course. What if I started a petition? Would you sign it?'

'Well . . . I don't see why not. As long as it's all legal and above board and everything.'

'I'll make sure it is, don't worry,' she says firmly, not having a clue what she's talking about or letting herself in for.

She thinks about it all morning. It doesn't tug her mind away from work but it drifts in every time there's a lull. The idea of a man with a gun patrolling the streets against foxes fills her with dread. Whoever this man is, she hates him already. She hates the way he makes his living and every stinking thing about such a person's sordid miserable life.

She can't let this happen. If she loses the fox, she might never know what it said to her that night. She has to stop this from happening.

She has to stop this from happening again.

She passes Winston in the main corridor in the lunch hour and they both stop. He has his hands in his pockets and seems deadpan and aloof.

'I enjoyed last night,' she says, cringing at herself, hoping no one heard that remark, including Winston.

'Me too,' he murmurs. 'I gotta go though. I got a lunchtime band practice an' I'm runnin' late. See you, Miss.' As he's walking away, he turns around and adds, less stiffly: 'Maybe at the gym.'

It seems he isn't completely 'off' with her, as she feared, after all then.

In the staff room she finds Roz Lincoln about to start her lunch.

'Hi. Roz.' The younger teacher looks up at her with mild curiosity, wondering what Amy Trent might want with her. 'Sorry to interrupt but I wondered if I can have a word with you about one of your music students. Winston Paige.' She notices Roz become visibly wary.

'Why, what's he done?'

'Nothing. Well. Look, I don't want to interrupt your lunch . . . '

'Well if we can't talk here,' Roz says, discreetly indicating the other staff, 'let's go and find an empty room. You got sandwiches?'

'Yes,' says Amy, holding them up as if to prove she isn't lying.

'We'll take them with us,' says Roz, wiggling her Tupperware lunchbox in the air. She's young and a little peppie and has years of saying 'OK' ahead of her.

In the nearest classroom on the ground floor they find a lone fourth-year boy with his head stuck in a Lee Child thriller.

'Sorry,' says Roz, interrupting the boy, 'but outside please. You're not supposed to be indoors anyway.'

The boy picks up his bag disconsolately and slopes out of the room without a word and they shut the door behind him.

'I understand he's a good musician,' says Amy.

'Winston? Yes, he's very good. Maybe even talented. He's been playing for a long time, mind, and I'm worried he might've reached a plateau. He's good but there's a lot better out there. I just hope he's got the growth to develop.'

'Got the growth? I'm not sure what you mean.'

'I mean that to develop as a musician he needs to be big enough as a person. He needs to be mature enough to take it to the next level.'

Again, Amy isn't sure what this last sentence means. The parsing of it is ambiguous: is being 'mature enough' a prerequisite or a driving force? She lets it go, watches Roz sit at a desk and open her sandwiches, then does the same herself.

'But you're not here to talk about music, I take it. Did he do something?'

'Why do you keep asking that? Is he the kind of boy to do something?'

'To be honest, yes. He can be. He can also be charming and— '

'Mature?'

'OK, yeah, sometimes. And sometimes not.'

'For example?'

'Now that wouldn't be fair on Winston. Ultimately he's one of the good guys and I'm not going to badmouth him over mistakes he made when he just wasn't thinking straight.'

She's half-talking like she's one of them, the students. Badmouth. One of the good guys.

'Mistakes,' says Amy. 'We're not talking about music are we?'

'No, but perhaps we'd know what we were talking about if you came out with it and told me what's on your mind.'

Amy bites the bullet and tells Roz about the incident in the Shakespeare class and describes her reaction to it as best she can. The only other teacher she's so far mentioned it to is Roger, and she hasn't spoken to any of her family or friends about it. She's only telling this young woman because she apparently devotes a lot of time to Winston in the music room as one of her star pupils, protégés, whatever, and therefore she might know something about him that can be useful in puzzling it all out.

'My God, I don't know what to say. That's awful – I can't imagine how you must've felt. But it's not like him. I've seen him in a lot of moods but I've never seen him be cruel to anyone. He can be moody if things aren't going right with the band but he's never had a go at anyone like that.'

'I don't think he was having a go though,' says Amy. 'He didn't say it to be cruel.' She pauses, wondering how much she can confide in this person she barely knows but expects to behave to professional standards. 'At least that's what he told me later.'

'So you've spoken to him about it?'

'Yes,' says Amy without elaborating where or when the conversation took place. 'He said something strange though and I wondered if you might have some information. He told me that he'd picked those quotes and said them to me as a kind of prediction.' Saying it aloud sent a chill along her spine.

'So he told you about that,' says Roz. 'He must trust you.'

'No, he wasn't happy about it. He said something about the other kids calling him Voodoo or something. After that he clammed up about it.'

'That was a while ago, they've got bored and stopped doing it, but it still bugs him if anyone brings it up.'

'Brings what up?'

'I'm surprised you don't remember it. Maybe it was before your time? 2005?'

The time reference makes her think about Roz's age: she must be quite a bit younger than her; she'll have come here straight from teacher training, they all do these days, nobody can afford not to.

'Before mine,' Roz confesses. 'I only know because he told me about it.'

Amy is getting the message about Winston's trust, how Roz has it and she doesn't, but she listens patiently.

'The 7/7 thing with the bus bomb at Tavistock Square,' Roz says.

Amy tries to think what she was doing that day but can retrieve no clear picture. The fog of memories of being with Colin, thinking herself back to a time when he was alive, clouds out the momentous day.

'Apparently Winston begged his mother not to get the number thirty bus that morning. She didn't and afterwards she called the newspapers about it and Winston's story ran on the inside pages of all the tabloids. The poor kid hated it. He'd never wanted to draw attention to himself.'

'So how does he feel about his mother?'

'I'm not his shrink,' says Roz tucking into cheese and tomato. Amy sips her orange juice, waiting for Roz to finish chewing. 'I think he's forgiven her though. He realises she didn't know what she was letting him in for at school.'

'Why did she believe him?' says Amy suddenly.

'What?'

'When he begged her not to get on the bus why didn't she think it was nonsense? Surely he was just a child. How old then? Thirteen?'

'Mrs Paige is a religious woman. Maybe it's connected with her faith. I do know though that it isn't the first time it'd happened.'

'What, the predictions?'

'The way he's described it to me, it's not so much a prediction as a premonition.'

'Is there a difference?'

'What I mean is, he doesn't see what's going to happen, he just knows something bad's going to happen.'

'And is it always bad? You said it's happened before.'

'I don't know the details,' says Roz, 'just that something

else happened sometime.' She tries to sound indifferent. 'He hasn't talked to me about it.'

So Winston's trust in his music teacher only stretches so far after all.

But Amy is thinking about something else now. She's thinking about the fox. Winston is now the one other person she knows who's also had what seemed to be some kind of paranormal experience. If she can get him to talk about it to her it might help her understand her relationship with the fox and what should be done about it. Who knows – he might even help her recover the words that Colin spoke to her the night that the fox found his voice.

23

The question has now become whether she, as a teacher, can trust Winston with a story that frankly makes her sound crazy. In her favour, Winston himself knows what it feels like to be ridiculed, and Amy believes Roz completely when she says he can't be cruel; and these are the first bricks in the architecture of her trust in him. But perhaps there's a way that will allow her to hold back her motive for wanting him to talk about his premonitions. She comes to a conclusion: the subject is clearly a touchy one for him, so to get him to open up she will have to strike a bargain with him – trust for trust. For him to talk about his experiences, uncomfortable as it will be, she will have to offer him something in return.

She looks out for him all afternoon in the school corridors between classes, intent on arranging a meeting for them to talk, but she doesn't see him. Nor does she attempt to track him down: it would be a mistake to go looking for him and risk setting tongues wagging, either students' or teachers'. Considering what she wants to discuss, the less everyone else knows about it the better.

At the end of the day she hangs around the school gates for some moments, feeling adolescently foolish, before swiftly walking away from the suspicious glances of departing schoolkids.

She goes home and watches *The Weakest Link* and tries not to think about coffee granules or her reflection in the kitchen window or what the fox said to her or what Christine was about to say or what's on the tape that Max found, but she can't stop herself thinking about Winston and the things he said to her last night. Winston said the lines from Shakespeare constituted a prediction: is that what they represent in her dreams?

The news comes on, the new political scandal brewing over MPs' expenses that is encompassing all parties. Cameron is quicker off the mark than Brown to slap it down hard but it won't surprise her if he's at it too. All pigs at the same trough – an expression she recently read or heard somewhere, perhaps from another teacher. Everyone is pissed off about it. It's a public consensus as wide as that over the bankers last year. She was mad at the bankers all the more – perhaps a little more than she would've been otherwise – because Colin was so furious with them. He was going to grill Cameron about that in his interview. He'd be in fits about all this expenses stuff if he was here now. But he isn't, and she can't work herself up fully about it; she has too much else on her mind.

She cooks with disinterest something basic in the kitchen then eats it off a tray in front of the TV and finds herself wondering if Winston will be at the gym tonight. It's only a twenty-minute walk away and it's still light till nine. She could sit and wait in the coffee lounge with a view of reception, reading the health club's magazine like a character in an espionage film – George Smiley or Felix Leiter, the sidekick missing the real action taking place elsewhere. And then when – if – he appeared, pretend she was doing what? There's no yoga class tonight.

She supposes she can go swimming but that will entail actually going swimming since faking that you've been swimming is quite hard to do convincingly without at least a damp swimming costume and a smell of chlorine about you, and actually going for a swim will preclude the object of waiting and watching for his presence.

The phone rings, the land line. Her parents? When did she last speak to them? Guilt, guilt.

'Hello?'

It's Max.

'Amy, listen, I was wondering if I can ask you a favour.'

'What?'

'When I came round that time and searched Col's office I noticed some old photos of his. I wondered if you'd let me keep some of them.'

'Well – yes, of course.'

'I mean if they're not special to you.'

'No, I – that's fine. Where are you?'

'I'm in London. Is it OK if I come over?'

'What, you mean now?' She sees the prospect of speaking to Winston tonight start to climb out of the window.

'Would that be all right? I won't bother you for long.'

'No, it's not that. Yes, please. Come over as soon as you like.'

'About ten, fifteen minutes.'

It's a damn sight sooner than she anticipated but she agrees, wondering where he is now and what he's been doing. He seems to have friends everywhere; the chance is high she supposes that some of them will be in London. She glances around, checking to see if the place is a mess. A little – no biggie. He can like it or lump it. If he wants tidy she'll need a lot more notice than this. It's the second time she's thought that about Max. As if it's becoming a mental habit. She used to think the same thing about Colin whenever he caught her unawares with an invite to dinner with someone important he was trying to woo for the press: *If he wants me pristine and presentable he should've given me more notice.*

Christ, she isn't turning Max into some surrogate husband figure that she can hen-peck, is she? After all, she can hardly target Colin: it's hard to complain about a fox for its human failings and mean it.

She puts the kettle on. The comforting cuppa, always there to break the ice. Not that she expects ice but that, living in London, she isn't used to receiving visitors at home on a week night. The kettle boils long before he arrives. When she hears him knock at the door she switches it on again, conscious that she's wasting energy and feeling foolish over it.

'Come in.'

'Hi, how are you?'

They do the kiss, just the one side. She's glad neither Tunisia nor American Karen has introduced him to that confusing business of the double kiss, one to each cheek, that you never expect and invariably bungle.

'Kettle's just boiled,' she says, leading him to the kitchen.

'Coffee for me, please.' She remembers how he takes it. 'I hope I'm not intruding coming round on a school night.'

'No, I was just watching telly.'

'Expected to find you buried under a stack of marking or something.'

'I try and get it all done at school so when I come home I can forget about it.'

'Why, is it that bad?'

'No, it's not bad at all. Well, it's not all bad, put it that way. But I try to keep work and home separate.' The memory of being with Winston in the pub floods her with the kind of guilt that accompanies a lie. Max doesn't notice. He sips his coffee and makes some appropriate appreciative noises and the conversation moves on. 'So what've you been up to?' she asks chirpily.

'This and that. Driving around a lot visiting various people. Friends. Business. Met up with an old flame from years ago the other night. Went to the theatre with her. She had a spare ticket, someone'd cried off. All very innocent,' he adds for her benefit, 'no touching.'

'Would I know her?'

'No. Way before your time, from when I was still at school. She tracked me down through our ad for the diving school on Facebook.'

'Tracked you down, eh? Sounds like she's still interested.'

'She's married. Happily, I think. And speaking of marriage . . . ' Max pauses, waiting for a reaction.

'No!' Amy says at last, knowing what's coming.

'Is that shock or disapproval?'

'You and Karen?'

'We've been talking about it for a while.'

'You're getting married? I don't believe it.'

'It's the right time. Mum and Dad are going through a rocky patch at the moment and I think a wedding will be a good way of bringing them together and helping them see sense.'

Surely, she thinks, it should be a way of bringing you and Karen together, but she reckons that might be the wrong turn to take in the conversation right now.

'I'm sensing this isn't about Colin,' she says, meaning whatever is troubling his parents.

'No. I don't think so anyway.'

'Oh God. Well what's it about? Haven't they said anything to you?'

'They're playing it close to their chest. You know what Dad's like. Tight-lipped. And Mum, well, I'm afraid she's the suffer-in-silence type and I'm sure you know that too.'

'She's too humble for her own good, that's Christine's problem. Don't you have any clues?'

'I think it might be something Dad's done. Mum's got

that put-upon look and he's skulking around like a dog that's wet the carpet.' Amy laughs. 'To be honest, I've only stayed there a couple of days at a time, then I've been off again. I love them but I can only take them in small doses, then I need a break for a few days.'

'You must be spending a fortune on all this travelling around.'

'I just hope the business is going well. Karen says everything's OK. We'll worry about the credit-card bill later.'

'Hey, listen, I'm sorry to hear that about Edward and Christine. D'you think there's anything I can do?'

'I dunno. If I think of anything I'll give you a call.'

'So am I going to have to buy a new swimming costume for this wedding in Tunisia?'

'Ah. Well. A swimming costume might be a bit inappropriate in London.'

'Karen's coming over? When?'

'Pretty soon. In about three weeks.'

'Oh my God. Is the wedding booked already?'

'We're working on it. Registry office just down the road. You could walk to it from here. But we'll get you a car.'

'This is unbelievable. Your parents must be pleased about that.'

'They don't know yet so don't say anything.'

'No, of course not.'

'I'm waiting for the right moment when it's all finalised.'

'I understand.'

'Now about those photos . . . '

'Oh. Yes.' Amy puts her coffee down and springs into aimless activity. 'Where did you see them?'

'In Colin's office. In a shoe box. I can go get them and we can look through them together, see if there are any you want to keep.'

'What are they photos of?'

'Me and Colin, mainly, from when we were growing up.' Max is careful to say 'mainly', hoping it will slip by.

'Oh no, just sort through them and take whichever you want. He'll have scanned most of them to his laptop anyway, I can always look at them there.'

So there is a laptop.

Max leaves Amy in the kitchen finishing her coffee and preparing to fill the dishwasher and enters Colin's study. He knows this is where he saw the picture he's looking for but can't remember which box it's in so he has to sift through a couple of them before spotting it. He takes that one plus some of him and Colin and other family members taken eons ago. He slips the first one into his back pocket then replaces the boxes and returns to the kitchen.

'It's just these few, hope that's all right,' he says, holding out the ones in his hand. 'Wanna show some to Karen.'

'No worries,' says Amy not even bothering to look, busy gathering dirty cutlery. It looks to Max as if she's let it pile up for a few days, not that it's any of his business.

'Right.' He drains his coffee mug, watching the constantly moving shape of her back as she busies herself at the work surface. 'I'd best be getting along. Unless you need a hand.'

'No,' she says, turning round to face him, 'this'll only take five minutes. Then I'm going to have a foam bath with candles and a glass of wine followed by an early night with a good book.'

'Right. Well.' Amy watches his Adam's apple bob up and down. 'I'll leave you to it then.'

'That's great news about the wedding,' she says, wiping her hands on a tea-towel and moving towards him. They do the kissing thing again, clutching elbows. 'I can't wait to meet Karen.'

She doesn't come outside to wave him off because he's parked down the street. When he gets inside the car, he pulls the photo from his back pocket, the second item he's stolen from their home, though technically the tape wasn't stealing, just felt like it.

He turns on the dim overhead light to have a better look in the encroaching twilight.

The picture shows him and Colin a decade younger, both in dress suits, posing in front of a large white hotel somewhere in the countryside in the English summer sunshine. He can't remember who took it. As a keepsake it's nice enough, sure, but what really interests Max is the sign on the front of the building behind them, announcing its name, which he'd forgotten.

The Devonshire Arms.

He checks his wristwatch. It's getting late to be thinking about driving out there now. He'll leave it till tomorrow. Once he gets the road atlas out he'll remember how to get there.

24

Amy wakes the next morning feeling guilty. Once her head clears she knows immediately what it is out of all the things it could be – her initially selfish response to Colin's accident, which still nibbles at the back of her mind; the fact that she still hasn't started her campaign to protect the fox yet even though it was on her mind so much yesterday morning; half a dozen other things she's either fretting over or putting off for no good reason. No; it isn't any of these. It's Edward and Christine. If what Max said is right about some kind of ruction in their marriage why hasn't she noticed anything? But as soon as she asks herself this question she realises that the signs have been there plain for her to see all along and that she has wilfully failed to interpret them.

She thinks about Christine's reluctance to socialise after the visit to Colin's grave and what confessional remark may have been rising to her lips when Max had entered the room that morning. Then there was Edward's not being there. That was odd for the weekend he knew she was coming. But this is all in retrospect. What she feels guilty about is not acknowledging these signs for what they were at the time because she was so wrapped up in her own concerns – what with Winston and the tape and the fox: Colin.

It is Colin – she knows it.

Maybe she should make an effort to forget about all of these questions that seem to be dominating her life and drawing her deeper into social isolation. Maybe she should stop regarding them as questions. Maybe that isn't the way forward. Maybe she should stop worrying about the past and live her life as it comes, only looking forward. If Winston's gift is premonition – though his litany of quotations seemed more to represent a prediction than a premonition, by Roz Lincoln's definition – then that's where she'll find the answers: in the future, in the fullness of time. By worrying about it so much, by trying to rush towards the answers, she is unconsciously wishing her life away. Not just her life. Wishing time to speed up means shortening everyone else's life too, though no doubt Roger, with his science magazines, would attempt to disprove it: time is relative to the observer and all that. What strikes her about that theory is that nobody has the time it would take to make the tedious and eternal observations that would empirically prove it. If the prevailing circumstances render a hypothesis irrefutable then they also render it useless, or suspect at best.

She makes the decision to focus on immediate practicalities. There's Colin's wardrobe to clear out still – or is she going to let his clothes hang there indefinitely like exhibits in a museum? Death isn't an infection: there are people who'd be happy to get some use out of them if she took them to a charity shop.

She needs to work through his files on the laptop too. They're all there in folders visible on the desktop; she's switched the machine on and glanced inside them several times, reading the file names and not getting any further than that. She knows his work habits: what isn't active, part of an ongoing assignment, he would save to a memory stick or to the PC in the office and delete from the laptop's hard drive. It's only a notebook, nicely portable but with limited capacity, and he was fastidious about freeing up memory.

None of it will be relevant now. As stories, she assumes they're all dead, well past their sell-by date, but she should sort through them to check. If there's anything that seems to be of use or interest she should pass it on to one of Colin's friends or colleagues, pick a suitable name out of his address book. Then she'll delete the lot so she can either use the machine herself or consign it to a good home.

She resolves to make a start on these chores today when she gets home from work and spends the best part of the day looking forward to getting to grips with them, feeling optimistic, that her plan of action represents the turning over of a new leaf. The proof of course will be in the doing. Every day has its agenda of good intentions but few of them end in a clean sheet. What was it some sporty guy once said on the telly? Focus, focus, focus – which is all very well when it isn't the bloody telly that's distracting her from focusing.

Winston hangs back at the end of that afternoon's Upper Sixth English Lit class. She idly wonders, her mind chasing clichés, if it's his sixth sense that told him she wants a word with him, then brings her thinking up short when it strikes her that it's precisely his sixth sense that she wants to talk to him about. His real sixth sense. If it isn't that which has stopped him leaving, is he really some teenage wolf in adult sheep's clothing making the most of his opportunities? It dawns on her that she might have to watch him. He may only be eighteen but he's a big athletic lad.

She finds him taking the conversational initiative, sees herself on the back foot in a space that she should be in control of.

'If this is about the hoodoo voodoo thing—' he says, despite her having indicated no reason to detain him. Then suddenly they're speaking over one another till it's hard to tell their own voices apart.

'It's not. You're the one hanging around. How did you know—'

'You're the one who was bringing it up the other night.'

This isn't a teacher-student conversation: she has a deep sense that it shouldn't be going like this.

'Wait,' she says. 'Calm down a minute. Please.'

He stands there, waiting. She judges it better to say all she has to say in one piece while she has his attention.

'The other night in the pub you said you'd love me to see your band—'

'I said I'd love to play to you,' he interrupts, bringing her back to what he'd really said.

'Yes. Well I'm offering you a deal. I agree to come and hear you play if you do something for me. The reason I want you to do something for me is that I've been having some unusual' – she almost says problems – 'experiences lately and I can't think of anyone else who might be able to help me understand them.'

'You mean me? I can help you?'

'I know it's something you don't like to discuss. That's why I'm offering something in return.' His face sours a little. 'Before I say anything else, I'm not asking you out of idle curiosity, and I'm not taking the piss. I know you've been through a bad time with it—'

'Miss, I know what you're talkin' about so you can stop beatin' about the bush, you know. You wanna ask me about my "predictions".' He says the word with the needling tone that another kid making fun of him might use. 'What you wanna know about that stuff for anyway? You know as much as anyone else round 'ere.'

'It's— It's a bit odd. A bit embarrassing, maybe. It's nothing like what happens to you. It's very different. But it's something weird. Something I can't explain. Yours is the only experience I've got to compare it with.'

'Well, what is it?'

'I'd rather we didn't talk at school. Not about this. We need to find somewhere.'

'Were you serious?'

'What about?'

'Letting me play for you.'

'Yes, of course.'

'Then I've got a suggestion.'

'Go on.'

'My family are away this weekend. Driving up to see relatives in Leicester. Big family get-together. I got out of it to stay at home and revise for my exams. Bit of peace and quiet to myself, like. If you come around say Saturday evening or summink we can have our talk an' afterwards I can play you some tunes, show you some a my moves on the keyboard.'

She senses herself near the edge of something she wants to back away from.

'Oh, now, coming to your house . . . I'm not sure that's such a good idea.'

'Miss, you said we'd struck a deal. The band's got no gigs lined up – I can't see another chance coming up until after the exams. It's hardly a million miles away from where you live—'

'How do you know where I live?'

'You said it was near the Wetherspoon's. I'm guessing you live near there.'

'Yes. Sorry.'

'Come on. I'll make some food, nothin' fancy, nothin' formal. No sittin' at the table or nothing, just some food and a chat and me playin' some a my music.'

What does she have to fear? As long as he doesn't know her address. Maybe she went a bit over the top about that. If she wants him to trust her she has to show reciprocation. But she isn't sure that it's a conversation she can have in his home. She doesn't know how it will go and she will hate to create bad memories associated with the place where he lives.

'I tell you what,' she says, 'meet me somewhere else first to talk then we'll go back to yours for the music afterwards.'

'That's askin' a lot a trust, Miss, if you know what I mean.'

'I promise. OK? I just think it'd be better to get this – subject off my chest first. Then I'll be able to relax and enjoy the music more. I just mean meet in a park or a pub or a coffee shop somewhere where we can get the serious stuff out of the way first.'

'A'ight, that's cool. What time?'

'Five, six?'

'Make it six on Saturday. There's a snack bar place at the end of our street. I'll write down the address.' He leans over her desk and, picking up her pen, writes with it on her notepad. 'I gotta run now, Miss, I'm late for IT.'

'Tell Mr Parker it was me who kept you.'

'Thanks, Miss.'

'Thank you.'

25

After school she resists turning on to *The Weakest Link* and gets to work on Colin's wardrobe instead. It suddenly makes her wonder if Max has been through the pockets. She can't remember specifying that. When she comes across a note on a scrap of paper in the hip pocket of his old blue jacket, then more in other pockets, it suggests that Max didn't search them. As she sifts through, the little notes accrue in a pile. She'd forgotten that he used to do this; not forgotten exactly but been reminded. After she's finished the long process of removing everything from its coat hanger, folding it neatly and laying it carefully in a plastic sack, the trousers and shirts building layer on layer until the sack is full and the drawstrings are drawn tight and tied in a knot, she gathers up the wad of retrieved paper and takes it downstairs. It has been quite a long job and she needs to eat before she goes on to the next task. She puts the notes down on the work surface beside her in the kitchen and starts preparing some food. When she looks in the cupboard the easiest option that stands out is spaghetti. There's a fresh jar of passata lurking at the back there too. She chops and fries an onion and a sliced courgette with some crushed garlic then adds them to the passata in a saucepan before stirring it into the boiled and drained spaghetti, the whole lot then sprinkled with basil and cracked pepper. There's half a bottle of red wine left on the side from a couple of nights ago. The pasta put her in the mood even though it was early for it, only seven. She removes the stopper and sniffs at the neck of the wine bottle and it smells fine. She carries the bottle with one hand and the food on a tray with the other into the living room and sets them down before returning to the kitchen for a wine glass. As she's reaching up to the cupboard she sees the pile of creased and folded papers from Col's pockets. She picks them up; she can look at them while she eats.

Out of habit, she switches on the TV before settling to eat and out of habit she flicks through the five terrestrial channels and rejects sport, *Emmerdale*, teenage soap and a grinning talk show before resorting to *Channel 4 News*. Some people consider it a duty to keep up with the news and know what's happening in the world, or at least the country, which is fine except she thinks that so little of what passes for news matters to her that the duty becomes ridiculous. Half the news is advertising in another guise. The duty isn't to an idea of citizenship, the duty is to an ideology of consumption. But it's the best thing on – and she wants the television on. Not out of habit but of a desire for company. Given the human singularity of her domestic life, it's the next best thing to a cat – or a fox. That is her civic duty: to save the fox. She will get onto it at the weekend. Another project to keep her focused on the now and the future.

Having finished the dish of spaghetti in record time she takes a slurp of wine and picks up Col's notes. He was always jotting down ideas on old envelopes and scraps of note paper then stuffing them into his pocket and forgetting they were there. He never needed to look at them again: it was the act of writing things down that fixed them in place in his brain. She thinks of the number of times these fallen leaves from Colin's mind have spoilt a good wash load by flaking apart in the tumble and suds of the washing machine.

The top one that she reads first is a to-do list – everything from phone so-and-so and finish such-and-such to 'pay C/C bill', 'oil change' and 'buy coffee'. Nothing ticked off but all of it done, she bets. She doesn't know if the coffee was a jar of instant or a Starbucks. She can easily picture Colin jotting himself a reminder to pop into a Starbucks but instead an image of coffee granules comes into her head. She puts the list aside, starting a pile that can be chucked straight into the recycling. The next is a two-sentence outline for a piece about the GLC and the current mayoral system – which has served London better? She remembers that one; it became a two-page feature in *The Economist*. She adds it to the recycle pile and moves on.

After five minutes the recycle pile has attained a certain stature and remains the only pile. This is all redundant, unimportant or indecipherable stuff. Some of it, without context, resembles little more than meaningless drivel. None of it is of any obvious value. She is about to toss the rest of it on top when the last scrap she glances at contains just a name, 'Craig Sefton', and as her eyes read it the same words, 'Craig Sefton', come to her ears from the newsreader's voice on television. The moment quickens her. She bolts upright, almost spilling her wine, and zaps up the volume.

The screen cuts away to a filmed location report: men in suits shaking hands, the flicker of flashbulbs, then a balding politician speaking from a podium. It's a story that is neither something nor anything about a non-event at which the man in question is addressing the press but she watches it long enough to find out who he is. It's nothing more than a mildly spooky coincidence – her reading the note and hearing the name on TV at the same time, the chance meeting of two events, like Colin and the log – but she finds herself unable to overlook it. Craig Sefton – a shadow junior minister and one of the front-running golden boys to emerge *Anno Cameron* from the Tory rank and file. The report ends without her knowing clearly what it was about, a meeting of some trade committee or something, but the name Craig Sefton is starting to ring a bell now.

Quickly, she clears the debris of dinner away to the kitchen then goes and gets Col's laptop, returns to the settee with it and switches it on. Once it's booted up it doesn't take her long to track down what she's looking for. It's inside a folder named 'Pieces' within a larger folder named as the current year and which is right there on the desktop. She goes into the 'Pieces' folder and there it is, a file labelled 'Craig Sefton'. When she double-clicks the mouse on it she feels like she's sitting shoulder to shoulder with a ghost. The feeling is fleeting. When the document opens, she finds herself looking at a template for what she can only describe as a dossier. Like something out of James Bond or *Man From UNCLE* or the murky Whitehall of John le Carré. A dossier on Craig Sefton. It's headed with a slab of biographical details, name, age, birth place, education, the various positions he's held in his political career – all very boring but curtailed, selective, a sketchy beginning of the fuller document it might have grown into. At the end of the biog is a section headed in bold type 'Action', but it's empty except for one sentence: 'What's he up to?' She scrolls down, looking for more to go on, but there's only empty white space. Just that one question. *What's he up to?*

She closes the file and sorts through the rest of the paper notes that she'd discarded without reading, looking for anything related or otherwise important in its own right. One bears the initials 'TJ', which mean nothing to her, others just dates with no places, phone numbers with no names, scribbled on lemon-coloured Post-It notes, the white insides of carefully peeled beer mats and the backs of store receipts. Satisfied that they are all discardable, she puts them on the recycle pile and turns back to the one she's kept.

She's half afraid that if she looks at it again she'll hear the name again. It's only a short step from that to imagining it was really Colin reading it out over her shoulder. She folds it in half and puts it to one side, without having a clear idea of why; just the timing coincidence, which spooked her, and thinking that that question in Colin's dossier on Sefton is something that another journalist might still be interested in investigating.

26

He's always liked Miss Trent. Amy now. Outside school. Her
rules. He's always known of course that Amy is her first name
since as far back as he can remember her coming to teach at his
school. It's one of those things that spreads around straight away
every time a new teacher appears. They don't all like it – some
don't seem to give a toss – but their first name is always the first
snippet of info to circulate with the sly hope that something can
be made of it: winneting after a suitably comical nickname.
Trent, her married name, pathetically turned to Trout for a short
time but soon reverted to Trent when the irrelevant cruelty of
Trout failed to catch on. Nobody can think of anything to make
from Amy other than a pitiable hamster joke that also quickly and
mercifully dies the death. In fact the name Amy is kind of sweet
in an older generation way. In an older woman way.

He doesn't know what it is about her but there's always
been that something that attracts him. One time it was the
fullness of her lips, another the way she had her hair tied up in a
green headscarf. She's clearly old, at least thirty, and he likes that.
He's seen old movies from the Seventies like *The Graduate* and
The Bitch with somewhere in the story an older woman who
knows how to take charge of a younger man in the one place
where it counts. And the media is always heaving with top class
older women. They're everywhere. Who is there? Kylie
obviously. Joanna Lumley. Catherine Zeta-Jones. At the top end,
Joan Collins – she's doing all right for her age, he saw her on a
chat show the other night where she could've passed for twenty-
five without the bright studio lights. And Helen Mirren. Look at
Helen Mirren. She must be about seventy to be able to play the
Queen like that in a film his sister made him watch on telly one
night some time back and she still looks good in the papers in a
bikini.

But that's all irrelevant. Amy is who she is, and being an
older woman just helps. He knows she was married but the
husband never once showed his face to pick her up from work, he
knows that for a fact from the day he started watching her. He
knows what the guy looked like from his photo in the papers
when he died and he was never seen with her in or near the

school grounds anytime during the last two years for sure because he would've been the one seeing him.

He remembers between classes wandering onto floors and down hallways where he had no business being because he could catch sight of her every Tuesday and Thursday walking fifteen feet along a corridor out of one classroom and into another. He remembers dusky late-autumn afternoons with school coming out – this was when he was still in the fifth year – watching his friends who were going the same way as him walk away and leave him behind waiting for Miss Trent to exit the building just so that he could watch her silhouette against the shining bronze of the setting sun walk the length of the school yard and out through the gates. He was enraptured. Before long he was in the habit of walking out behind her at what felt like a discreet distance and following her to the nearest Tube station where he stopped, finding it hard to justify pursuing her underground. His only object was to keep her in his sight without her noticing. Because if she asked him what he wanted of her, he would have no answer.

Those sad-sack days of tailing her around are over now, but he still doesn't know what he wants from her. He doesn't know what he wants from any female, apart from the obvious. Sure, they're useful, they can do jobs as well as men and all that shit, but they're still a different species. Women are from Venus, men are from Mars and all that shit. Except of course he's sure they aren't all like that. Amy isn't like that. Miss isn't like that. Funny that: Miss when really she's a Mrs. They call all the women teachers Miss. Maybe there's a song in that for the band.

When he got put in her sixth form English Lit class it was like all his Christmases had come at once. It meant he could be close to her and be looking at her without having to skulk around the school gates anymore. And it gave him the chance to talk to her, if he ever found the guts or, failing those, another way. He was sorry for her when her husband went and carked it over a cliff, they all were. But through all that time there was something that niggled him. He never really put his finger on it until after he opened his fat mouth and said what he'd said in that Shakespeare class. And it was this. Her husband never once came and picked her up from school. Wasn't he supposed to be a freelance journalist, meaning he basically had no full-time job, and yet he didn't have just one free afternoon in his schedule to just one time come and pick his wife up from work? She's a fine lady. She didn't deserve that kind of neglect. What kind of fool would call that a happy marriage?

Still, he never meant to say what he said. It was some force that drove him to it. He had a long list of quotes printed out and lying on the desktop in front of him and he was darting glances at it wondering which to choose and they were the ones that flew straight into his eyes and out of his mouth.

In some ways though it was a good thing. Damn, it's one of the best things that's happened to him, music included. It brought him into her world. His marginal position in her world had been fixed until that moment. He'd been just Winston Paige, that black kid in the third row. The way he impacted on her consciousness that afternoon changed all that. Like in a Venn diagram. He recalls at least that much from maths or physics or whatever it was. Now their worlds overlap. She's part of his and he's part of hers. Not that he planned it that way. It's all because of something he said, something he had no control over. Now, instead of him wanting to talk to her, she wants to talk to him.

Can that be what these predictions are about? He hasn't had many, only four in his life that he can remember, but is there some progression to them that he isn't finding? Are they leading him somewhere? Is this where they're leading him? To her? To Amy?

27

She finds a print shop in the high street that will do her five hundred fliers saying SAVE OUR FOX in white block letters on a nice green background for twenty pounds. She nearly puts STOP THE KILLING but doesn't want to send out a mixed message that she is campaigning against hunting – not that she supports it. Anyway, she reflects in time, you can't stop killing that to her knowledge hasn't started yet. She makes up a petition letter on Col's laptop and manages to work out how to connect it to the printer in the office without having to phone anyone. Then she spends an evening walking the nearby streets knocking on doors, trying to reassure people she isn't selling anything and then angling for a way in with her pitch, or pushing one of the fliers through the letter box if no one is in. Trish Taylor is the first to sign the petition, obviously edgy at being the first name after Amy's and reiterating her concerns about gunmen patrolling the neighbourhood to persuade herself. She said she'd sign though, and going to her first girds Amy's loins for all the strangers she will have to sweet talk after. At the Binghams she's invited in for a cup of tea that she can't refuse and discovers that they like animals and travelled on a family holiday around the safari parks of Botswana last year, attracted there by the Mma Ramotswe stories. It's about as safe as you can get in Africa but it isn't cheap. There was a time when Amy would've been delighted to talk to them about travel but now it only reminds her of the long summer ahead, and where will she want to go without Colin? She steals a glance at the clock and collects all their signatures before announcing that she has to move on. She avoids the woman at number 34 whose cat got mangled. Maybe another time. By nine o'clock she is exhausted as she returns home with a fistful of remaining fliers and a list of twenty-six signatures including her own. Not an overwhelming number but she will go out again tomorrow night and the night after that until the weekend comes.

She rises earlier than normal on Saturday and phones her parents, thinking the hour will give them a shock. Mum is out doing something horsy but she speaks to Dad. He sounds cheerful but she knows him well enough: it's the chipper tone he adopts to obscure something not so cheerful inside. Others might miss it, even Mother sometimes, but not her, though the nature of what's troubling him is something she fails to winkle out.

She tells him about the fox. Not that it's Colin, she spares him that, but about its presence in the gardens and her campaign to save it. He says how glad he is that she's keeping herself busy, which of course makes her feel she hasn't been busy enough, though he would never intend it as a rebuke and would be upset to think she'd taken as such, which of course she hasn't. It's comforting to speak to him, especially since she's learnt of Christine and Edward's troubles, though she doesn't raise that with him, not wanting to be the one to start any inter-family gossip.

She hangs up, gratified by the chat but bothered by what can be on his mind that she read in the stoical tone of his voice. She doesn't allow herself to ponder it long. If it's another question in that long list of questions, another piece to the puzzle of – of what? – it will have to get in line with the rest of them and wait. The fullness of time. The present focus on the now and the future. The rest can wait. Don't they understand that she needs to find herself before she can find them?

She keeps herself busy through into the afternoon, not letting herself feel guilty. After lunch she takes a bath and starts thinking about getting ready to go out. She won't wear a skirt, though good practical skirts are what she favours most of the time. She should wear trousers tonight. And a top that doesn't reveal anything either above or below. Does she have time for it to dry if she washes her hair? She can twist it up in a scarf. What the hell is she doing planning her wardrobe already at two o'clock in the afternoon? All she wants with him is a private conversation and here she is behaving like a school girl going on a first date. In the end she goes with the scarf, the bright green one she wears to school sometimes. It feels suitably teacherly, grounding her in a professional frame of mind.

The afternoon is bright and he was right about the walk, it isn't far, half an hour. She gets there ridiculously early and takes a window table in the appointed caff, a greasy spoon run by a friendly and vociferous Turkish family. While she waits for Winston with a mug of milky coffee in front of her she rehearses what she wants say to him about the fox and knows it will all come out differently.

When six o'clock arrives and he isn't there a premature wave of doubt pulses through her to the core. Two minutes of reigning in her impatience later, the door jangles open and in he walks. His clothes look new, crisp, all trendy labels she's never heard of, and he smells of lotion, as if he's just showered and freshened up at the gym.

'Hope I didn't keep you waiting,' he says after ordering something she doesn't hear at the counter.

'I got here early,' she says.

'I've got some food ready for later. Is that all right? You haven't eaten already?'

Amy can sense he's as nervous as she is.

'No, I haven't eaten.'

'You ever tried jerk chicken?'

'I've eaten it in the Caribbean.'

'No way. You have been in the Caribbean? You know you like it then. I made some a that with rice an' peas.'

'Sounds good.'

'Well, I'll be honest, I made it last night an' I was gonna heat it up tonight in the microwave so I don't know what it's gonna taste like but I don't think it'll poison us.'

'It'll've given the flavours more time to come out.'

'You mean like leftover pizza always tastes better the next day.'

'Yeah,' she laughs, 'something like that.' Standing at the giddy edge of their serious conversation, she is suddenly feeling as if she can have fun with the boy.

One of the proprietor's daughters arrives with Winston's order, which appears to be a cup of lemon tea.

'So come on,' he says, 'we might as well get it over with. What's this thing you want to talk about?' He blows on the surface of the hot brew to cool it and Amy catches the reassuring lemon scent.

'Before I say anything you've got to promise me one thing,' she says in a level voice. 'You've got to promise me you won't laugh. If you laugh I'll walk out. And I haven't paid yet.'

'All right,' he smiles, 'I won't laugh at you so long as you don't laugh at me.'

She draws a deep breath.

'I've been visited by an animal recently – a fox, actually – and the other night it spoke to me.'

'A fox? What do you mean, it spoke to you?'

'I mean it said my name. I mean, I heard it say my name.'

He isn't laughing but she can see he's having some trouble with it. 'You mean it really talked? It talked to you in English?'

She pauses not adding anymore yet, awaiting his judgment.

'That is weird. It's not just weird, it's double weird. How did it know your name?'

'I think I know who it is.' It's hard for her to say the next bit after all that's gone before. 'I think it's my husband. I think it's Colin.'

Winston needs a moment to take this in, not saying anything but looking straight at her over the table, perhaps looking for signs of a wind-up.

'Do you believe me?' she says at last.

He ignores her question and says, 'Did it have his voice?'

'I'm not sure. It's all a bit vague. It was Colin's style. I don't know about the timbre.' Winston can sense the self-consciousness in the way she says the French word, as if he might not understand it, but he lets it pass. 'We talked for a while but I can't remember what we said. It was all a bit overwhelming. I mean, a talking fox—'

'Who's also your husband.'

'It sounds crazy, I know.'

'Are you sure it wasn't a dream?'

'It wasn't the first time I'd let it in the house. I can remember the first time clearly. And the second time was no different. Except it didn't run straight out the front door. It stayed and – talked.'

Another pregnant silence falls between them as the hubbub of the café swirls around their ears.

'When I was twelve,' says Winston, 'I can remember a mate of mine down the street lost his mum in a car accident and a couple of months later his dad bought him a puppy an' he became convinced that it was his mum reincarnated. He worked out it musta been born on the day she died an' he believed it. So did his two sisters. They all believed it, they didn't make a secret of it.'

'This fox is too old. It must've been alive before Colin died.'

'Well there are other possible explanations. Some cultures believe that humans have some kind of animal spirit inside them, don't they? Like the North American Indians. Maybe this is his spirit living on in some form. Maybe it passed into the body of your fox.'

She finds it hard to swallow the idea of Colin of all people coming back as a fox, though evidently that's what's happened. She has never, though, entertained the notion of the fox being his spirit represented in animal form. She knows that it was Colin because it talked like Colin and seemed to know things that only Colin would know, like her name.

'What does it want?' she says. 'Does such a thing have a purpose? A mission?'

'I dunno, Miss. Amy. Sometimes these things can signify some kind of warning. I think I read that somewhere but I'm not sure, I could be just making it up.'

'Have you heard of anything like it before? Talking animals? Spirit walkers?'

She was preparing herself for the excuses, the rational explanations – the ridicule. It has to come sometime.

'I know that animals have communicated with me in ways I can't explain. Just before I had a prediction once, me and our old dog, Luther, exchanged a look across the kitchen an' I knew right then for some reason that he knew what was about to happen to me. There was something about the way his eyes grabbed my attention and then he gave a little flick of one eyebrow right before it hit me. It was just a little raise of an eyebrow, the old Roger Moore routine, but I knew it was significant. He knew something. It was almost like he caused it, it was like that – boom-boom, one after the other, like cause and effect. That was the morning I saved her from the bus bomb, my mum.'

Now it was Amy's turn to be silent for a beat.

'But you've had others,' she says, 'more of these' – she substituted the word tentatively – 'premonitions.'

'A few, yeah, before that one. First one I can remember

134

was when I was five. I was sitting playing with my toys on the sitting-room floor and I looked up at my mum and says to her, "Mum, Sally's gonna get hurt." Sally's my little sister. Turns out she'd managed to crawl out the front door and was about to go for a wander in the traffic. I don't know how I knew, I just did. No one made much of it at first, it was just an entertaining story at family gatherings. Then when I was eleven one day I got a really bad feeling about my Uncle Jimmy. I didn't see anything but when it happened I kinda blacked out, it was like for a second the room got sucked in around me and everything vanished into a black hole. I kept telling my mum that something bad had happened to Uncle Jimmy. She wouldn't listen at first but I convinced her I was serious an' she phoned Jamaica. Turned out while I was watching *Buffy the Vampire Slayer* Uncle Jimmy was getting shot to death in a bar somewhere in Kingston.'

'Christ. That's awful.'

'I know. My mum went down for the funeral on her own. He was her brother. Dad stayed at home with us kids. We couldn't all afford to go.'

'How did you deal with it? The premonition. How did your family deal with it?'

'They're religious. They think it's a gift. That's OK. It means they're cool with it, they're not gonna lock me up in a mental hospital. But it scares me. I don't know when it's going to come. And why me? It's a responsibility, you know? I never asked for this shit. I'm scared what I'm gonna see next.'

'But it was a blackout.'

'Yeah. That time. The next time was much worse.'

'The bus bomb.'

'Yeah. There were visuals that time. I saw my mum' – there was a catch in his throat and he swallowed it down – 'screaming an' in flames. You know, the kind of thing you might force yourself to think about sometimes to make you more careful around the house or to make you love her again after a row or something. We all have some horrible thoughts sometimes about people we love because we wanna be ready to protect 'em and we force ourselves to go there and look at 'em in the worst situations. But when it just pops into your head from nowhere it really puts the fear of God in you.'

She prays that he's being figurative and that this isn't

135

going to turn into a pitch for religion.

'So no,' he concludes, 'apart from budgies and parrots, I don't know anyone who's seen a talking animal except you. It sounds implausible but then look at me. I still don't know how I can help you though.'

'Is that all of them? The visions, the premonitions.'

'You mean you. Apart from you. That's the only time since my mum. That time in the Shakespeare class.'

Amy is quiet now, waiting.

'A sorry sight,' he says.

'What?'

'A sorry sight. That's what I said. In the classroom.'

A sorry sight. My God, she'd forgotten that.

'That's what I said, innit?' he asks. 'But you did look a sorry sight. I felt sorry for you. I felt sorry 'cos I didn't want to watch you waste your life. You looked – I dunno, like you were wasting away. I couldn't bear to watch it.'

'That other stuff, the truth will out, the naked truth, all that stuff. What truth?'

'I dunno. Lookin' back, it was just – a lot of embarrassing nonsense. I have no idea what I was tryin' to say. I just said it. I wasn't even thinking clearly. I'm not thinking clearly now. I'm just sorry I opened my mouth. I'm sorry.'

'I was hoping you might suggest a way to help me recall what the fox said that night. I have a feeling it might've been something important.'

'Maybe music might help. You describe your experiences with the fox and I'll bring it to life on the keyboard.'

'Are you serious? Can you do that?'

'There's only one way to find out.'

28

They pay up and leave and walk down the street to the Paige family house: a slightly larger terraced house than her own in a less expensive part of the borough with a front yard adapted for parking the family car that is, she supposes, on a street in Leicester right now. She wonders what his parents would say if they knew about this; somehow she doesn't imagine that he told them she was coming round. It could look a bit rum, the teacher coming home with her young pupil on a Saturday afternoon-stroke-evening. Avoiding Winston's notice as he goes in ahead of her, her eyes dart about looking for nosy neighbours before she slips inside hurriedly behind him without looking back.

'My keyboards are up in my bedroom,' he says turning round towards her on the stairs. 'I hope that's all right. There's nowhere else to keep 'em. Then we can come back down an' have something to eat.'

'Straight to business then,' she says, wishing she hadn't and following him up the stairs.

'Oi, just music business,' he snaps back cheekily.

His room is in the attic and the big blank end wall of it is covered by a Jamaican flag with a depiction of Bob Marley's benign, dreadlock-framed, iconic face on it.

'Oh, don't mind that,' says Winston. 'I used to be into me Bob Marley when I was a kid. We still use some reggae influences in the music but deeper, fatter vibes, you know what I mean? Marley nowadays sounds a little too jiggy.'

He sits down at a keyboard and flips a switch and various bits of it light up in vividly attractive blocks, strips and blobs of glowing colours. Another two keyboards are set up on their stands, one of them ranged above the one he's sitting at so that his hands can switch between them and the other within reach to his left, combining to fill quite a significant portion of the room's space. She looks at the dark stacks of speakers occupying most of the rest of it and the name plates crowd around her – Marshall, Fender – conjuring bands she went to see play live in her twenties. Winston leans over to reach another switch and an amplifier thumps to life.

'So what's it like when the fox comes?' he asks.

She picks up the thread of the rehearsed narrative, somehow expecting his musical response to be jokey, a cartoon interpretation of a fox with a Disneyesque human personality. Instead the notes tinkle in from a picturable distance, pattering quietly and cautiously about and making her see the fox the way she watched it explore her garden. As she describes its approach to the house, the electric piano evokes the sure rhythm of the fox padding up to the windows and intersperses it with short striking flits from one tempo to another and other flourishes that match the fox's unpredictable stops and starts.

'That's amazing,' she laughs, forgetting the fox now in marvelling at his talent as he lifts his hands slowly and calmly away from the keys. 'That was truly amazing.'

'Hey, you're gonna like this one,' he says and turns back to the piano.

She recognises it as soon as the choppy notes dance in and laughs at herself for not already having guessed what was coming.

'"So What?"' she calls out.

'By?'

'Ronny Jordan.'

'Courtesy of me, courtesy of Miles Davis,' he says taking a bow to her applause at the end of a few bars.

'Play some more,' she says with a child's greedy excitement.

'I swear, Miss, you put a blindfold on me an' I'll play this thing like Ray Charles or Stevie Wonder, an' you get to choose which.'

'Let's skip the blindfold and you just play something else.'

'All right. But on one condition. You go over there and sit on the bed and relax. You're making me nervous standing behind me. Go and make yourself at home.'

'OK, OK, but play something else.'

She slips her shoes off and settles onto her side with her knees up on the mattress and her head propped on one wrist.

'So which is it to be?' he says, looking across the room at her, at Amy, on his bed. 'Ray Charles or Stevie Wonder?'

'Mmm, Stevie Wonder.'

'You're sure? You sure you want Stevie Wonder? 'Cos

138

this is serious stuff now so you sure you want Stevie?' She giggles. 'OK, you asked for it.'

She doesn't know it to begin with. There's a whole prelude that he's made up himself. Then the chords modify to the familiar key, taking up the familiar melody. Then he starts to sing.

'My cherie amour . . .'

He sings in a deep, rich voice that takes her by surprise. It's controlled and appealing but it doesn't lay on the treacle. None of that *X-Factor* warbling and fussy arpeggios. She's only guessing at what an arpeggio is but she knows that she likes what she's hearing. It's simple and soulful and he makes her feel like he's singing it just to her. This is her performance. She feels a little foolish. She's out of practice at absorbing such close attention. When the song comes to an end she's able to grin and clap and resume normal service.

'That was beautiful, thank you.'

'It was always either gonna be that or "You Are the Sunshine of My Life".' Something about the words – as if he's foreseen this moment, or planned it – make her listen with fresh ears, and make him fall silent after all the giddiness, as if he's suddenly given the game away. 'Maybe we should take a break an' go an' get something to eat.'

'Yes,' she says a little reservedly, 'I think we should.'

It's only halfway downstairs that she realises she hasn't put her shoes back on, they're still up there by the bed. Would it make a difference to her life if she turned around now and went back up for them? But she can't go anywhere without them, so she shakes off the sense of a pivotal moment and continues down the stairs with Winston descending behind her.

'In the sitting room, there,' he says pointing the way. She opens a door into a room that is kept airy and fresh but not spartan, soft furnishings aplenty to provide comfort. 'We haven't really got a dining room. I hope it's all right to eat it on trays.'

'That's what I always do.'

'Great. I'll go stick it in the microwave. Take a seat. Do you want me to put the telly on?'

'If it's no trouble,' she says, thinking how lovely telly would be right now to distract them both from oneself and each other.

He leaves her with the early evening news and disappears into the kitchen for ten minutes. Every so often she hears the *ting* of the microwave bell. She's half reading the titles on a bookshelf and half listening to the noises of him serving up onto the plates in the kitchen when that name leaps out at her from the TV again. Craig Sefton. Cameron is on the screen being asked who he'd want in the Cabinet under a Conservative government and the fact that Sefton's name comes up is clearly of some significance to the on-the-spot reporter's agenda judging by his comments over the end of the interview footage.

'I got you some wine,' says Winston in the doorway holding up a bottle of red. 'I know you like Merlot. I hope that's all right.'

'Well,' she says, her mind still on the TV, the sudden intrusion of that name into the room like an uninvited guest, 'yes but just one glass.'

'Is something wrong, Amy?'

'No, no,' she says pulling herself together. 'Merlot's fine. It's perfect. You go and bring the food and I'll open the wine.'

The chicken tastes wonderful, spicy but not too hot, and the wine is an inexpensive Australian that she approves of. With the television droning in the background she lets him talk while she pours herself more wine, noting that he is drinking something non-alcoholic but warming too much to the idea of a second glass of Merlot to give it a second thought.

'I like you, Amy,' she listens to him say. 'You're not like anyone else. You're not one a the bitches.'

'Don't use that word,' she says turning on him viciously.

'That's what all the kids use. Even the girls sometimes.'

'And who do the girls get it from?'

'The boys. I know all that, I ain't stupid. But why do boys call girls bitches?'

Because they don't know any better, she wants to say, but knows it to be trite and unhelpful. *Because they're boys*. Her mind tears through the anguish of finding the right words.

'Because they're boys, and until they stop saying it and thinking it, they'll never be men.'

'You can't stop them thinking it though.'

'Oh no? You can if you stop them saying it. Have you never read *Nineteen Eighty-four*?'

She hopes that doesn't sound patronising. That's not what she intended. She's talking to him as a friend now, and he is supposed to be a literature student after all.

'Is that George Orwell? Wasn't he a communist?'

'Does it matter? Not that he was. Read it and you'll find out. Trust me. You'll love it.'

'It's not gonna brainwash me with secret hidden messages or nothing, is it, 'cos if it is, man, I'm tellin' ya – '

It's a joke of course, and a good one. This whole evening is pleasantly turning into the good joke that finally negates the bad joke that began all this, and the memory of the incident finally disintegrates once and for all under a hail of friendly fire. She sees something else though being constructed in its place and she doesn't know whether to tear it down now or see what kind of architecture for the future it might raise between them; and anyway, she knows that to tear it down now, to commit such wanton and cruel destruction, she can summon neither the words nor the resolve to do.

She pours another wine and lets herself dip and swim in the flow of his talk until it's later than she thinks, and then Winston vanishes to the kitchen and returns with another bottle of wine.

29

When she wakes up she doesn't know where she is. It's a sensation she hasn't experienced for a long time, not since the morning after that first night in the tent in France, which makes it doubly disorienting. She reaches across the bed instinctively, lifting her head off the pillow and stretching open her eyelids, and her hand comes into contact with warm human flesh. Her brain is still too groggy to immediately revolt and instead begins to accommodate the result of what must've happened last night, some of which is coming back to her.

Winston's body stirs under the touch of her hand on his shoulder. It's as if he's primed to respond, sleeping only ever the shallow sleep of the constantly alert. He sits up stiff and looks at the bedside clock. For a second she watches him panic.

'Oh, shit. I thought it was gonna be later than that. Thank God.' He squirms back down into the bed beside her. 'They shouldn't be back for another few hours. Thank God you woke up. I woulda slept there till noon, easy.'

Amy is still acclimatising. What memories she has of the night before fall into order, leading up to the big here and now. Intuitively, in what feels like a dream, she slips a foot out of bed to get up.

'Whoa,' says Winston, 'wait a minute. I said they won't be back for hours. We don't have to rush. We can take five minutes.'

His arm is slipping around her shoulders, but neither proprietorially nor questing for sex. It seems he just wants to hold her a while longer. Like it could be the last time. Should it be? This should never have happened in the first place but there's no point freaking out about it now. She has to be rational and adult, part of which means owning up to her own role in this. It must've been something she wanted: she can't think what she would really be doing here otherwise. The thought of visiting any other student's bedroom is something she would never allow to occur to her, yet here she is, not just thinking about it but already having done it. And more, a lot more, besides.

Talking foxes! What kind of lame excuse must that have seemed to him?

Amy rolls over onto her side until she's facing him, then leans in and kisses him on the lips. She lets her mouth linger, secretly enjoying it, but won't let it develop, pulling away as soon as he begins to seek her tongue with his.

'I've got things to do. Besides, I want to leave enough time for us to at least have a cup of coffee together before you kick me out.'

He relinquishes her with a smile and she sits up, having to combat a little wooziness but capable of dressing efficiently on autopilot.

'You don't wanna take a shower?' says Winston.

'Why, do I smell?'

'Well no but—'

'I'll do it when I get home. It's no biggie, a'ight? Now you go take your shower and I'll go put the kettle on.' She's up now and hopping about in one shoe, searching for the other.

'You know where you are, right? Just go straight down the stairs and at the hall turn right to the kitchen.'

'I'm a big girl,' says Amy, finding the lost shoe and sliding her foot into it, 'I'll work it out. Where's my handbag?'

'I ain't seen it. You sure you brought it upstairs?'

'Yeah, I'm sure I had it in here last night.' She spots it on the floor by a cupboard and bends down to pick it up.

''Cos you had a lot to drink last night.'

'What's this?' Amy asks.

'What?'

She stands up.

'This.'

The clingfilm-wrapped brick of weed she's holding in her hand.

'Look, just put that back, a'ight?'

'This is a dealable amount. Are you dealing?'

'Please. Amy. Please put it back. You shouldn't have touched that.' She shouldn't even have seen it.

'I'll put it back when you've answered the question. Are you dealing, Winston?'

His only option is to talk his way out of it. They both know it.

'How else do you think I'm gonna pay for all this stuff? Whatever little I make sellin' weed goes on this. Music's my life.

My parents don't do too badly but they couldn't afford all this.'

She isn't even going to address the question of where his parents might think he gets the money from.

'And this is all of it, all your profit?' she says gesturing at the instruments across the bedroom. 'How long've you been doing it?'

'Since I was thirteen.'

'You smoke it yourself?'

'A little here an' there. Not much. Like I said, it goes on the music.'

'And is being stoned part of your music? Is that how you let yourself go?'

'Yeah, sometimes.'

Amy stays silent for a while. Then she puts the brick back on the ledge in the cupboard and closes the door that was left ajar.

'I just want you to answer me one question,' she says, straightening her jacket and pulling her bag onto her shoulder. 'Have you ever sold any at school?'

'No, Miss.' She looks hard at him. 'No, Amy, honest. A couple a people have asked for it but I won't sell it at school. I need to keep it separate from that otherwise it wouldn't work.'

Amy's hand is on the door. 'Jesus,' she says, 'no wonder you see things.'

'That's not fair,' he says, and though it's the obvious protest, she knows that she's hurt him. He's right, it wasn't fair, but this isn't the time or place to go into that now.

'I can't have anything to do with this. I'm sorry. I'm not going to see you outside school anymore. Do you understand?'

'Amy—'

'No. I'm not getting mixed up in it.'

'It's not getting mixed up in anything.' He is still in bed, propped up but naked under the duvet, vulnerable, unwilling to expose himself further. 'You're not gonna say anything, are you?'

It's too pitiable to be a threat, more of a plea.

'Like I said, I don't want anything to do with it. So who would I tell?'

She opens the door and goes through it.

'Amy—'

She looks back though she knows she ought not to. She looks back and her gaze takes in the musical instruments, the Bob Marley banner on the wall, the little cupboard containing the block of cannabis, Uncle Jimmy gunned down in Jamaica, the young black man stranded in the bed pinned down under the cover of the duvet by his inability to reveal his true self beneath. It's a place, a world, she has no business being a part of – and she wonders why she hasn't seen something like this coming all along. The gangster's moll, the 'Sweetie' stuff – she never wanted that in real life and she doesn't want it now.

'From now on it'd be better if we stuck to Miss,' she says before walking out on him, before leaving that world behind.

30

She spends the rest of Sunday locked in the house with the land line off the hook and her mobile switched off, wondering what the hell she thinks she's been doing. He's an eighteen-year-old boy and one of her students and she got drunk in his family's home and slept with him then found out he was mixed up in gangs. For God's sake, he's half her age.

She takes a therapeutic bath and forces herself to eat some brunch, limiting herself to one cup of coffee because it will only stimulate her brain more. She tries to read a book but her mind keeps coming back to the new problem, the new *thing*, that she's created for herself. She switches on the old 'Sweetie' film and tries to watch that and by the time it's halfway through she's tearily leafing through the albums at photos of Colin, not maudlin but rather hating herself for her stupidity. It's another of those Colin-would-never-do-that moments, like the thoughts that flutter around the elephant-in-the-room presence of the thing on the tape.

The worst thing of all is that the sex is coming back to her now. On first awakening it had been fogged over by the shock of seeing where she was and the alcohol still in her bloodstream. Now the fog is clearing and images and memories keep looming out of it into full or partial mental view. Her willing nakedness. His body next to hers on the mattress. His penis in her hand. His penis in her cunt. There; she says it – in her mind at least: cunt. Like one of those word puzzles in the papers. From *cunt* to *slut* in four moves altering only one letter at a time. It looks so easy but she spends ten minutes trying to work it out in her head before her mind gives it up as not possible, and returns to self-flagellation.

She spends a restless Sunday night trying to stay asleep until the dawn chorus from the street convinces her that it isn't going to happen. The next thing she knows, she's was waking up and it's eight o'clock already, half an hour past her usual rise and shine. She must've forgotten to set the alarm. There's still plenty of time to get to work but she's had such little sleep she knows she'll be no good to anyone today.

It's as good an excuse to herself as any. She phones in

straight away before she can talk herself out of it and leaves a message on the office ansaphone telling them that she's unwell and not coming in and what work the supply teacher will have to set. Then she goes back to bed. Everyone deserves a sicky now and again, and she doesn't want to confront the real reason why staying away from school seems like such a good idea today. She wonders how Winston will react in class when he sees she isn't there. She wonders if Winston will be there himself.

Later, after she's slept off some of the exhaustion and her mind has had more time to absorb the facts of her situation, she thinks that writing something down might help. Help with what, she isn't sure. Her conscience? Some kind of verbal exorcism? Fear of committing anything to paper or, God forbid, a computer document, where some clever dick can always find a way to retrieve it, drives the idea away.

She sets herself to reviewing the fox campaign as a form of distraction and a signifier of moving on. She counts the signatures on her petition and maps out the streets she's yet to cover. In the evening she even forces herself out of doors and onto her rounds. If her brain has to spend all its time obsessing over the same thing then at least her body can be walking around doing something useful. She may as well fret outside as in. The interaction with people – strangers – keeps her momentarily occupied at each door she visits, but her vulnerability antennae are up all the time. Could Winston be around here? They live within walking distance of one another; conceivable walking distance: this is London, not Texas. Something might bring him innocently or otherwise to this part of town. Or there is the other possibility: she never established to her satisfaction, she now realises, that Winston doesn't know exactly where she lives.

In short she doesn't know whether this is a situation that developed out of Winston's ostensibly uncontrollable outburst in the Shakespeare lesson or whether it developed out of a deeper, longer obsession whose compulsion the boy might've been under, to what extreme she can only guess. He could've been following and observing her for months, years even. She isn't so old that she can't remember what it's like to be a teenager with an infatuation. She was infatuated with one of her own teachers as a sixth former and imagined all sorts of ways that the paths of their lives might intersect outside the confines of the school world.

The difference is that she didn't try to make it real. If you want to make it real, write about it. Set it down. Write poetry or stories or songs or Valentine's verses. Use it however you like. But don't try to make it really real; don't try to make it come true. That can never happen. It only destroys the fantasy.

In between her internal wranglings with either Winston or herself, she campaigns with an uncharacteristically stoked vigour. After a few sharp discussions along the way with potential petitioners – Amy is prepared to explain and defend her position to the point where she knows they aren't going to sign and no further: thank you very much, move on – she strides home with sore feet but a very creditable number of additional signatures collected. She's working up to taking this to the local council and the local press now. Surely there's enough to make it newsworthy to at least the local *Advertiser*. That's something she can start to arrange tomorrow. And thus a reason to take Tuesday off as well as Monday presents itself. A two-day sicky is more convincing than just the one day after all. No one gets over a cold or a bug in one day: it makes good sense. She can also make that phone call to her parents that she's been putting off, but without telling them she's off work or they'll be making a fuss over her, Dad worried, scanning for a profounder emotional undercurrent, and Mum disapproving – the sort of woman who would never have taken a day off ill in her life if she'd ever had to work one, and doesn't see why anyone else should. For the first time since Colin's death Amy's life is moving back into areas that she feels are none of her parents' business, and though the shift is calamitous in its causation she can also view it positively as another of those signifiers of things moving on and a new life accruing.

She's spent Sunday trying to sober up in more ways than one, and decides to lay off the wine through Monday evening too. It's one thing she can feel virtuous about. Instead she settles down on the sofa with an oversized mug of hot chocolate and a film on the telly with the lights down low. It's a warm night so she decides to leave one of the French windows open, at least until the moths and mosquitoes start flying in.

It must be around ten when she realises she's dozing off, and flexes her eyes back to the light of the screen. As she tries to work out how much she's missed and what's happening in the story now her line of vision shifts to one side and she becomes aware of a shape that oughtn't to be there in the darkness at the far end of the room.

It's the fox. It's inside the house, its haunches concealed among the pot plants from behind which its head and shoulders peek out. It's stock still and looking at her, watching her watching TV. When Amy sees it she just manages to suppress a flinch reaction in time. Now her eyes are connected in a sight line with the eyes of the fox and she keeps them there, worried that the tiniest of movements will send it bolting back outside. She ignores the light and colours flickering on the TV screen and keeps her eyes on the fox, watching, waiting, barely breathing. Waiting for and willing it to speak.

The fox remains silent and still. Occasionally its ears might twitch and its jaws shift or its head crane an inch further out from behind the potted palms. Amy keeps her eyes still, not even blinking . . .

Then she's waking up again and fifteen minutes have passed and the fox has gone. She stands up and goes with dwindling hope to the window to see if it's still in the garden. There's no sign of it and she shuts the window against the insects and locks it for the night. It's good still to know that for a short while maybe, Colin was there in the room watching over her as she slept in front of the TV.

31

When she finally switches it back on the next morning, her mobile phone ding-dings with a text message. She opens it with a slight dread, wondering if it could be from Winston. She can't remember ever giving him the number but he would've had access to her phone sometime during the fifteen or so hours that she was in his house if he'd wanted it. Instead it's from Max, but the words do little to put her any more at ease:

We need to talk. Pls call me asap.

We need to talk. Another of his Americanisms – one which has crept into standard British English through the bad, shorthand, written-by-numbers dialogue of the TV soaps. Talk about what? Naturally, only one topic comes to her mind that could command the tug of such necessity. *The thing.*

After a moment's hesitation she calls his mobile from hers, cradling it to her ear while she pours morning coffee – pretending the day is commencing as normal.

'Can I meet you after work?' Max asks.

'I'm not at work,' she says automatically, wondering if she will regret divulging the information later. 'I'm – I've been ill.'

'Are you OK?'

'Yes, yes – nothing serious. Just a cold.' She's explaining too much.

'If you're at home,' he says, 'is it OK if I come over?'

'I was planning on coming out to Berks this weekend. I can call round then if it can wait.' She means to his parents' house but already she feels disingenuous: she knows it can't wait or he wouldn't have sent such an ominous text.

'That's probably not a good idea,' he says.

'Why not? What's it about?' She tells herself there's stuff she needs to be getting on with, that the house is a mess, that she could do without the intrusion, but she knows she will say yes.

'It's better face to face.'

'All right. Come over. I'm not going anywhere.'

'I'll be there in the next hour or two.'

'Phone me if I don't answer the door. I might be out the back.'

She keeps herself busy pottering round the garden pulling up weeds, pruning bushes and searching for traces of the fox. She knows where it gets in and out and that the wildlife experts from the telly would no doubt be able to catch its scent, but she is unable to detect so much as a single fox poo to betray its presence last night.

When Max arrives she can't resist mentioning it to him, about its coming into the house while she was dozing in front of the TV. The anecdote provides a way of forestalling whatever it is he's come to discuss, and for a while he plays along with it.

'I didn't know you had foxes,' he says as she pours him coffee.

'They're all over London now. I think it's wonderful. I'm trying to stop some of the neighbours getting the pest controllers in though. I'd rather have foxes than the neighbours' cats and dogs shitting everywhere.' From his silence and the way his eyes shift about the kitchen she can tell he isn't all that interested. 'Let's go through to the living room.'

The good summer weather is still holding. She opens the French windows, as if preparing her escape route.

'Have you spoken to your parents at all recently?' Max asks her out of the blue.

'My parents? I was about to phone them when you rang me this morning. Then I put it off.'

'Oh?'

She finds this an odd thing for him to say.

'Why "oh"?'

'Nothing, I was just . . .' He lets the sentence trail off and it unsettles her even more.

'Why? Is it about them?'

'What? Is what about them?'

She's getting a little annoyed now. He didn't come here to skirt prettily around some unspecified topic. One of them is going to have to come out with it.

'Whatever it is you've come here to talk about.' She pauses, leaving him an opening that he doesn't take. 'I assume it's something to do with that tape. Whatever it was you found among Colin's things.'

'The tape?' – this said as if he's forgotten about the tape, as if it's the last thing on his mind. Damn it, surely he must know it's the first thing on hers. What's he playing at? 'Oh – no, sorry. No, it's nothing to do with the tape.' At least he's admitting now that there is an 'it'.

'I wish you'd spit it out.'

'So you haven't phoned them?'

'No, not yet. Unless you tell me what's going on I might have to. I don't mind telling you you're starting to freak me out a bit.'

'I'm sorry, I'm—' Max picks up his coffee, puts it down again without drinking, picks it up again. She's never seen him looking so fidgety and flustered. 'I'm not making much sense, am I?'

'Look,' she says. She reaches out and touches his wrist, guiding the hand holding the cup down to the coffee table. 'Put that down for a minute and focus. This is something I'm not going to like, isn't it?'

'Not much,' he admits, letting go of the cup. 'When did you last speak to them?'

'My parents? Why are you so concerned about them? They're all right, aren't they?' Scenarios of sudden death or injury flare in her mind. 'What's happened to them?'

'Nothing. No, they're fine – as far as I know.'

'I talked to Dad about a week ago. Maybe less.' She feels a sudden need in the face of Max's concern to be accurate now, and finds it is beyond her. 'It might've been last Wednesday.'

'How was he?'

'He was fine,' she says instinctively. Then it dawns on her that he isn't just asking out of politeness. 'He was—' It comes back to her now. 'He was worried – about something. I think. I didn't ask him but I could sense something.'

'What about your mother?' There is a curious edge to Max's voice.

'I didn't speak to her. She was off at a horse race or something. You know what she's like.' It's a rash thing to say – maybe he doesn't. Why should he? Maybe she's confusing him with Colin.

'Like my father,' he says; then adds, 'Fucking horses.' The expletive strikes her with the shock of a slap, leaving her momentarily at a loss for what to say.

'No,' she finally responds, 'not my thing either.' His

152

silence lengthens uncomfortably and he stares down at the brown surface of the coffee. 'I suppose it's a generational thing. Or the Countryside Alliance. All that.' She knows she isn't making any sense but she has to say something.

Max keeps looking intently at the surface of the coffee until she expects it to start rippling and bouncing telekinetically. It's the same look he directed towards Colin's coffin at the graveside during the funeral.

'They're – fucking.'

Amy is trying hard to follow.

'The horses?'

'They're having an affair.' His eyes move, latch on to hers.

'Who?'

He won't say it, just keeps looking into her eyes and willing her to see. When she does finally, she emits a little laugh.

'No.' He just keeps looking at her. He isn't smiling; if anything he's frowning now. It's a look that tells her this isn't a joke. 'No.' She says it again, fearing he hasn't heard her the first time. Still he says nothing. Still his eyes don't move from hers. 'No.' *Third time lucky*, a voice whispers at the back of her mind; but there is no such luck, no such sick joke to make it all right. 'It's—' The term that would spring to her lips to explain it away fails to arrive. It should trip off them without her even having to consciously produce it, but it isn't there. It's what? A mistake, a misunderstanding, absurd – or just plain disgusting? How could she know any of that? Where there should be animated defence against his accusation she is left instead as breathless and stony and silent as Max himself is.

'I'm sorry,' he says at last. 'I thought you needed to know but I didn't want to be the one to have to tell you. No one should have to tell you that.'

'How do you know?' she asks. Already she's thinking about the thing that Christine was about to say the time before the three of them visited Colin's grave, and her odd behaviour that day. She remembers now that it was when she hinted at the collusion between her mother and Colin's father over the David Cameron thing. But it couldn't have been going on then, could it? She'd have noticed something surely. Something in her own mother. Something in her own father.

Oh God. When she looks back now, it seems an obvious mess that she's deliberately ignored, to wallow all the more freely and luxuriantly in her own problems.

'Mum's been awfully depressed lately. It took a hell of a job to get her to talk about it. And' – Max can't bring himself to use the word *Dad* – 'he's been no help, just keeping himself isolated. I finally got some sense out of her yesterday. I couldn't believe it when she told me she thought it was Marian.'

Her mother's name jumps at her like a street mugger: identity confirmed.

'How does she know? How does she know it's my mother?'

'She says she's had her suspicions since before the funeral. I confronted Dad and he denied it of course.'

'So it's not confirmed. We don't know for sure.'

'I know that Dad was lying. Or at least being evasive. You can tell these things.'

That sounds like an accusation to Amy, even though she knows he doesn't intend it as such. He could tell so why couldn't she? The old self-recriminations flush through her brain pan.

'But it's not confirmed. It's a suspicion, that's all.'

'Then it wants confirming,' says Max insistently, his voice carrying an edge of anger. 'Or disproving,' he adds with concession. 'One way or the other. It's driving Mum up the wall. It's driving me up the wall. I can't go away and leave them like this. I can't do anything until it's sorted out.'

'It's wrong, it's all wrong,' says Amy. 'Someone's got their wires crossed. That's what it is. They just can't be—' She can't finish the thought because she can't contemplate it. 'They can't. It's not possible.'

'I know. I thought the same thing myself,' says Max. 'And we can sit here telling ourselves that until the cows come home or we can find out what the fuck is actually going on.'

Amy knows he's right, that this has to be sorted and that they are the only two around to do anything about it. She also knows that she doesn't have the stomach for it. In fact the very thought of it is one more thing that makes her feel sick.

32

Deciding to phone Alice is thinking outside the box. They don't speak often. It isn't that Amy's sister or any member of her family is *persona non grata* or *incommunicado* or any other Latinate term of which she has only a slippery grasp compared to Colin's. There is no history of bad blood between them. Quite the contrary; there is no history. Not really. Not recently. A childhood history, yes, but since then Alice has gone her own way, forsaking higher education and gainful employment to make babies. She and Colin used to visit them in Norwich for a while until it became clear that the visits were never going to be reciprocated. There was always something with Alice, usually involving the children for an excuse. She can't remember the last time they came south to spend Christmas with her parents, for instance. But that's fine. They have their own cosy family life up there and as long as Stuart isn't beating her that's fine. Not that he ever would. Poor Stuart, of course he wouldn't. He's a total sweetie really, what with all he will have to put up with from Alice, who's always had a capacity to be both demanding and commanding: taking after their mother, while Amy liked to think of herself as being more like their father.

When she gets her on the phone Amy is careful about what she wants to give away, keeping her concerns sketchy, inviting speculation, which she tries guide in her mother's direction. In fact, Alice knows less about their parents' current problems than Amy, which doesn't surprise her; but she is able to add some information.

'Are you suggesting what I think you're suggesting?' she says to Amy. ''Cause I know she can be a bit of a randy old sod.'

'Er – we are talking about our mother?'

'Oh yeah. What about those swingers' parties in the Seventies?'

'What swingers' parties? What swingers' parties? I never heard about this.'

'Jesus, Amy, she told me one night. She'd had a bit to drink – this is years ago. Her and Dad used to go to swingers' parties with the neighbours. What was it they called them? Key parties. Those car key parties. You know, where they—'

'Yes, I know what they are,' says Amy, 'I'm just not sure I wanna know.' A prickle of envy surges through Amy's body like electricity running through her veins: Mum spoke to Alice about sex but not to her. And Dad? Why would her father go to anything like that? It was hard enough to believe it of her mother; it was impossible to believe it of him.

She broods about it a little after the phone call is over, letting the old sisterly jealousies resurface unpleasantly. In working through and recovering from the sting it comes to her how she might be able to put what she has learned to some use.

33

She arranges to meet her mother in the OXO Tower on the South Bank. On the phone she keeps her reason for wanting to meet mysterious, steeped in suggestive confusion and daughterly neediness. If her mother knows her at all, which Amy knows she does, she'll know this isn't like her; Amy isn't the one who opens up to her – back in the day, that was always Alice. But she will also know that if Amy is free to meet her in the middle of a weekday then there must be a good reason for her to be missing work in the middle of term: the mystery, if nothing else, draws her in.

All it takes is one look at the ten-pounds-a-cocktail menu for Amy to confirm that the OXO bar is a little out of her own league. But her mother loves this kind of thing. The perception of opulence and the pretence of still being someone remains important to her and Amy has no real desire to burst that particular bubble, no matter what she may think of the woman, no matter how much she might abjure those particular values: the Countryside Alliance and all that, as she'd blithely put it to Max. The OXO Tower is evidently to her the new Ritz Tea Room and, as long as one can claim to account for all types, her mother will only remain stubbornly human. The teenage Amy would've hated her right now; whereas the thirty-six-year-old Amy coolly and rationally reflects that she hasn't actually murdered anyone.

'Were you planning to eat here?' she asks Amy as they stand next to each other surveying the view down the Thames towards the City. Suddenly her mother seems tall and athletic and faintly repulsive beside her. 'Only I've made other luncheon arrangements. I do hope you don't mind.'

Do you really? Amy wants to growl, but she resists the cheap temptation. She should give the woman a fair hearing.

'That's fine, no problem. I just wanted to meet for a chat really.'

Her mother orders an exorbitant round of drinks and they sit down at a table; the chords from a grand piano swirl around them. In a moment's abandonment of reason, Amy glances across the room to make sure it isn't Winston tickling the ivories, and feels herself redden a little.

'You know, I could've brought your father along. It would have done him good to get him out of that study of his.'

'What's the matter? Can't I chat to you for once without an intermediary?'

'Of course you can, dear, I've been telling you that since you buried Colin, God rest his soul. I just don't understand what all the secrecy is about.'

'Mum,' Amy interrupts, deciding to just go for it. 'We've never talked about sex.'

'Haven't we?' she says, and leaves it at that. She's stonewalling, Amy can tell immediately, but she isn't about to give up yet.

'I know you've talked to Alice about it; about – your own sexual experiences.'

'I don't remember.' She peruses a menu with sudden interest, not looking at her daughter. 'Is that what she says?'

'Look, it doesn't matter. I'm not – jealous that you didn't open up to me in the same way. This isn't about that really. It's—'

'It's what?' Her eyes are still looking down the list of expensive delicacies but Amy has her drawn her in now, into a conversation at least.

'It's just that we never talked about sex. And I think we're old enough now, don't you? And because for once in my life I actually want your advice.'

'Oh God,' she says looking up at last. 'You're not pregnant, are you?'

'Mother!'

'But you could've been. You know what I'm saying.'

'It's not Colin's if that's what you're thinking. What am I saying? There is no it. I'm not pregnant, OK?'

'But you've slept with someone. Since Colin . . . '

Amy detects an unspoken euphemism hanging over them: *since Colin passed on*, perhaps. She takes it as a statement rather than as a question, knowing this reaction will confirm its truth.

'Is it awful? Am I awful?'

'Of course not,' says her mother instinctively. 'Though it rather depends on who he is. I take it, it is a he.'

'Yes. But that's all I'm saying. I'm not telling you who

158

and I don't want to listen to any speculation on the subject.'

A waitress brings their drinks over and her mother's face maintains its blank composure throughout the manoeuvring of elbows and positioning of drinks mats. When the fussing has stopped and they're all settled, Amy gets in her pre-emptive strike.

'I'd like to ask you a personal question.'

'Go on.'

'Do you and Dad still have sex?'

If she expected her mother to spill her gin and tonic she was destined to be disappointed.

'That's a rather bald way of expressing it,' she observes drily, with just a hint of distaste.

'I'm not talking about love,' Amy pushes on provocatively, 'I'm not talking about making love, I'm here to talk about sex. I'm sorry if that's a little frank but that's really what I need to talk about now, Mum.'

'Yes, well calm down, dear, and don't make a scene, and perhaps we can discuss it quietly, like civilised people. I'm not being prudish, I'm being polite. The last thing one wants to overhear in public is two ghastly people baring their souls to a pitch that's embarrassing for everyone.' Her mother is right, she realises. She needs to calm down, to focus. Wherever the focus is or should be, she feels she has yet to find it. 'What's all this about truly?' her mother asks.

'I look at the future,' Amy says, 'and all I see at the moment is just me on my own and it frightens me. Yet the thought of playing the dating game . . . '

'Sounds to me as if you're coping with it quite adequately.'

'That's the thing though, isn't it? Listen to the tone of your voice. I can tell you don't approve. And I understand that. It's too soon. It's still too close to losing Colin for people to be comfortable with it.'

'If there's a point to this conversation, Amy, I feel we haven't come to it yet. I'm not sure what you want me to say, dear.'

'I suppose I want you to say that you understand. These days, sex isn't the object of the game, it's a strategy in it.'

'Now you're sounding hopelessly old-fashioned and out

of touch,' says her mother. 'And I still don't know what you want me to say. Go ahead? Sleep with whoever you like?'

'I want to hear you say that it's normal – that you have these feelings too, these desires.'

'No, Amy, you don't. You want to pry into mine and your father's private life without letting me pry into yours. That's what you want, though I can't think why, and I won't allow it.'

Amy tries a new tack.

'Dad's not happy. I can tell, and I want to know why.'

'Ah, here it comes,' says her mother, 'the accusation.'

'Is that guilt talking?' says Amy.

'Now that's enough. I won't have all this dissembling – certainly not from you.' Her mother looks as though she is about to stand up and leave. That would be just like her; she's barely touched her drink. The simple profligacy of it would be her kind of defiance. 'If you have something to say, say it. If not – well, as I said, I don't have all day to sit here beating around the bush.'

'Is Dad unhappy?'

'Your father is your father, same as he's always been. He's never happier than when he's wearing his air of melancholy. Ever the martyred old poet, that's your father for you. He doesn't need me to either do or not do anything to bring out his self-sacrificing side.'

The clue for Amy is in her mother's use of 'not do'; the implication of a service withheld. It seems to tell her all she needs to know about her parents' sex life.

'I'll let you go then,' says Amy, and drains her glass and clinks it down empty on the glass table top. 'I can see you're keen to move on to your lunch engagement.' She presses the weight of significance onto the last two words.

'I don't know what you want me to say,' her mother repeats, placing her faith in the statement of facts to smooth things over.

'I know,' says Amy, rising from the table. 'Don't worry. It's my fault. I thought we might be able to talk intimately, but it's something we never practised. I'm sorry, I should've known better. I'll get the bill for these.'

As she walks away she wants her mother to cry 'Amy', to call her back like in a million trite moments from *EastEnders*, a plea she can ignore with a false show of dignity. Of course, she knows it isn't going to happen and of course, it doesn't.

34

Outside the building she waits at some small distance where she can stand concealed from the exit. She feels foolish and conspicuous to the strolling South Bank crowds around her but she doesn't care as long as her mother won't see her when she comes out. She emerges a few minutes behind Amy and turns west, walking towards Waterloo. Amy waits till she thinks it's safe then starts to follow her along the riverside walkway, furtively hanging back in self-conscious cloak-and-daggery.

When her mother reaches Waterloo Bridge she mounts the stairs to the road and Amy has to hurry not to lose her yet lurk below the balustrade till she's certain she won't be seen. A couple of tourists eye her with obvious suspicion as she covertly observes her mother flag down a black cab heading north across the bridge. As it pulls away from the kerb she jumps out and is lucky enough to see another taxi approaching straight away. She waves it down, all too aware of what she is about to say to the driver and how he will take it.

'Follow that cab.'

'You 'avin' a larf?'

'No, really. Follow that cab, please.'

''S your fare, love.'

Her mother's taxi turns right past the West End theatres along Aldwych then left up Kingsway. Amy's cab is half a dozen vehicles behind in the sluggish traffic. At the end of Kingsway it crosses Holborn and proceeds up Southampton Row towards Russell Square. After a few moments it pulls over outside the Russell Hotel. By the time Amy's cab is able to stop to let her out, her mother is being ushered by a doorman through the front entrance.

OK, she knows where to find her now. She pays and thanks the cabbie then loiters for several minutes, keeping the hotel doors in view. Eventually she goes in, pausing on the threshold while the doorman continues to hold the door for her. Mother isn't in the lobby. She proceeds inside, and sneaks her way to the reception desk.

Amy slips a notepad out of her handbag, tears off an empty page and folds it in half. From behind the desk she's greeted by a smiling, efficient, uniformed young woman.

'Yes, madam, can I help you?'

'Yes, I wonder if you could. I need to leave a message for one of your guests.'

'Room number?'

'That's the tricky bit. I've only got a name.'

'I can't give out guests' room numbers.'

'No, of course not. But if I give you the name you can check if he's here and see that he gets the note.'

The way the young woman taps at the computer she seems to have no problem with that. 'What's the name?'

'It's Mr Edward Trent.'

The woman enters the name and looks at the screen. It takes her under three seconds.

'There's a Colonel Trent, first initial "E". Would that be the party?'

Amy swallows at the idea of a party up in that unknown room.

'Yes, that's him.'

'OK, madam, leave it with me and I'll put it in his pigeon-hole for you.'

'Thank you.' Amy hands over the empty, folded piece of paper. She considers pushing her luck and asking if a Mrs Marian Metcalfe is also registered as a guest, but the stretch of such a coincidence – that they both checked in independently of one another – and the subsequent futility of the question tell her to drop it.

'Shall I say who it's from?' asks the receptionist.

'That's OK, thanks,' says Amy trying to cool the heat of her emotions with pointed gratitude and forced politeness. 'He'll know from the note.'

35

That night there is a knock at the front door. Amy is in the front room typing up her publicity about the fox campaign on Colin's laptop. It isn't dark yet but it's later than she likes for unknown callers – almost eight o'clock. It will be someone selling dishcloths for charity no doubt, or persuading her to switch energy providers. The face on the other side of the frosted pane is obscured by low light. It could be man or woman. She slips on the chain and opens the door a few inches to peer through the gap.

It's a middle-aged chap with spectacles and a black woollen cap perched on the back of a head cropped close to mitigate male-pattern baldness.

'Sorry to bother you, madam. We've had some reports about problems with foxes around here an' I'm just going round gathering information.'

'Are you from the council?' Amy asks cautiously.

'No, I'm with a private company. We do work for the council sometimes but they're not my employers.'

'What kind of private company?'

'Pest control, madam.'

'Is it your company?'

'It's a family business actually, madam. But you have to be careful about that nowadays. We're a private company.'

'And you are?'

'Revill. Bob Revill. We're in the phone book, under the company name though. Here, if you're that interested.'

Bob Revill fishes in a pocket of his donkey jacket and pulls out a business card. He pushes it through the gap with black-nailed fingers and Amy snatches it without a thank you. She looks at it then looks straight at him as if matching the face to the information. Through the narrow strip of open doorway she eyes his body up and down, noting that he doesn't seem to be carrying a gun. But then he wouldn't, would he, until after dark, stalking innocent creatures in the dead of night.

'What do you want?'

'Just to know if you've seen anything or had any trouble; bins turned over, pets endangered, property damaged, that kind of thing.'

'No,' says Amy. 'Nothing like that.'

'Have you seen any foxes at all? Either on the street or in your back garden?'

'No. No, I haven't. And I'd like to leave it there, thank you very much.'

She shuts the door on him before he can protest and huddles behind it listening for his footsteps fading down the path. Now she knows the face of her enemy. But the encounter has left her feeling vulnerable and of all the people she might want to call on in time of need, curiously it's Winston who comes to mind; Winston that she is missing, Winston who would understand.

36

It's approaching crunch time now in the school calendar. No more free and breezy discussion about the whims and vicissitudes of character and plot. It's time for some serious work, and Amy has the lit exam groups practising writing exam questions under timed conditions in class now. It means a heavy marking load, taking it home with her. It also means much reduced interaction with the students in the classroom. She is invigilating, not teaching, while the students keep their heads down and scribble their little hearts out. Every time Winston submits his paper to her desk at the front and files out with the rest of them she resists the temptation to call out his name in another all-too *EastEnders* moment. While congratulating herself on keeping a distance between them, she's starting to feel that perhaps she was a bit too harsh on him.

But above all, she's terrified that word will get around the school, that she'll do or show something to give it away to the other kids in Winston's group: a look or a word that says more than it ought to. She's already having to take it on faith that Winston hasn't said anything about them to anyone, and won't. She's sure she could lose her job over it. It could conceivably lead to a court case even, and the dreaded newspapers.

When she finds herself thinking like this she reminds herself that Winston has as much to lose as she does; that she has knowledge over him too. But the thought, instead of reassuring her, increasingly makes her feel mercenary and dirty. Another day passes with the two of them avoiding so much as eye contact.

In the evening she prints out her letter to the council and the press, sealing several copies of the petition and its list of signatories in a number of separate envelopes and addressing them to their various destinations ready for postage the next day. Then she phones Max.

'I spoke to my mother today.'

'Oh yeah?' Max's mood is abrupt. 'Did she come clean?'

'Not exactly. Trying to talk to Mum about sex is like trying to talk to the Jehovah's Witnesses about gay pride.'

'You're not gay, are you?'

'Jesus, Max, that's what she asked. No, I'm not gay.'

'So, why did she ask?'

Amy stalls. 'It's a long story. But there's something else. I followed her afterwards. I'm sorry, Max, but I need to tell you this. She met your father in a hotel room.'

There is a long silence from the other end of the line but she doesn't hear it go dead. She waits, saying nothing.

'How do you know that? Did you see them together?'

'I saw my mother go in, and it wasn't for tea and pastries. Edward's name was registered to one of the rooms.'

Another silence, not quite as long this time.

'OK. Er, let's keep this to ourselves for now until I figure out what to do.'

'What do you mean, what to do? They're consenting adults. They're pensioners, for Christ's sake. They can do what they like. We can't do anything.'

'I mean let me see how things lie and I'll get back to you.'

'Where are you? Are you at home?' She presumes he will know where she means by home.

'No, I'm not at my parents' right now. I'll be back there tomorrow maybe. We'll maintain radio contact.'

'Max, this is shit. You know? I mean, when's Karen coming over?'

'Soon.'

'Do you really think this is the right time for a wedding right now, with all this going on?'

'Listen, Amy, don't freak. We'll see how things go. We'll play it by ear. Karen's a big girl. If we have to postpone, we can postpone. It's not a problem.'

'Does she know? Have you told her anything?'

'Not yet.'

'Why not? Doesn't she need to know? Don't you need to tell her? If Colin were here, I'd need to tell him.'

'I know, Amy, I know. But it's a little awkward. I don't want Karen starting off with a bad first impression of you.'

Amy feels her face glow and she tries to keep her voice from quivering.

'What d'you mean?'

'I don't mean you personally. But she's gonna see you as the link to "the other family".'

By that, he means *the other woman.* His tone clothes it in tactful quotation marks but Amy still feels hurt. Max is putting judgments into the mouth of someone who hasn't even met her yet. Why would he do that?

'Amy? You still there?'

'Yes, I'm still here.'

'Listen, I'll call you tomorrow and we'll meet up, talk about this properly face to face. I've gotta go.'

'OK,' she says trying to bestow some gravity to her pathetic whimper. 'Tomorrow.'

37

She tries to put Max's off-handedness out of her mind until the next time she sees him. She's helped by the distraction of a number of separate occurrences the following day.

At lunchtime, in the staff room, the topic of Craig Sefton comes up for discussion. It seems he's been in the news again, this time in a capacity that's clearly succeeded in getting real people, not just the media, to talk about him. She overhears some of it, not much, and doesn't join in, but it reminds her about Colin's dossier and its sinister question: What's he up to? She thinks about that all through lunch to no conclusion whatsoever.

Then halfway through the afternoon her phone vibrates during a lesson and when she looks at the end of the class, it's a text from her mother. Her mother never texts her. Her surprise at this is beaten into second place by the contents of the message: *OK, I'm ready to talk when you are.* Amy instantly recognises that this is no simple change of heart. Something has happened to make her send this. She starts putting two and two together. Can it be the empty note she left at the Russell Hotel? It would be easy enough for Edward to ask for a description of its deliverer then he and her mother will have put their own two and two together. She decides to ignore the text for now. It will be up to her, not her mother, to say when she is ready to talk again.

Finally, walking home after school, Amy spots Winston standing in front of a bookmaker's on the other side of the road. She almost crosses over then realises that he's with someone – a girl. Something makes Amy back up until a parked delivery van hides her from view. She takes a pace forward cautiously, hoping he won't turn and see her. It isn't a girl, she can see now. Well, sort of not. It's Roz Lincoln. The two are standing quite close to one another talking normally; there seems little animation or excessive body language to the conversation, nothing out of the ordinary, just two people talking. Then a funny thing happens. For a second or two, as they chat, their hands touch and linger. Amy is ready to be shot through with jealousy but she sees something that no one on the street is intended to see. To any passer-by, the touch of their hands would most likely have signified a gesture of friendly intimacy. But what Amy sees is something physical pass between them – an object, from one to the other.

So that's the special relationship between Winston and his music teacher: he's Roz Lincoln's dealer. Amy wonders how long she's been buying cannabis from him. Winston told her he'd been dealing since he was thirteen. Roz has been at the school for only two of those five years but it can easily have been going on since day one for all anyone knows.

Later that night she's still pondering this information and wondering what, if anything, she should do with it when there's a knock at the front door. Oh shit, she thinks, not again. She hopes against hope it isn't the fox killer again – what was his name? Bob. Like the demon in *Twin Peaks*. This time she doesn't open the door at all, even though the chain is already slipped across. 'Hello?' she calls through to whoever is outside.

'Hello, it's me.'

Max! That's a relief – until he staggers through the doorway. He's clearly had a few and, in concentrating on being careful, is noticeably unsteady on his feet.

'Are you all right? You didn't drive here, did you?'

'Nah. Got a cab. No problem.'

'Sit down, will you, before you fall down.'

'Hey, I'm not that pissed.'

She guides him to a sofa and he takes a momentary delight in sprawling himself out on it.

'Do you want a coffee?'

'I want a fucking drink.'

'That can be arranged, I suppose, if you're sure.'

'Hey, I'm not that pissed.'

'You've said that already. I've got wine.'

'Yeah. Wine, wine, wine. What is it they say? Wine and beer make you feel queer, beer and wine make you feel fine. That's the right order, isn't it? Beer then wine. I've had the beer so now I can have the wine.'

Amy goes and gets the bottle from the kitchen. She does it with some reservation but mitigates her misgivings by bringing a glass for herself too. Max takes the drink but doesn't taste it, instead waving it around gesturing with it as he's speaking, so that Amy, as she tries to listen, is worrying about red stains on the carpet.

'It's all fucked, Amy. It's all fucked.'

'Have you been back? Have you seen them?'

'It's bloody awful. There's just this – lumpy silence between them and when I'm there I'm stuck in the middle like a fly trapped in porridge.'

'Does Christine know you confronted him about it?'

'No. So I'm pussyfooting around behind both their backs. That's why I'm not there now. I've only been there an afternoon and already I had to get out.'

'Where did you go?'

'I came into London to see some mates. I just needed to chill out and forget about it for a while. It's doing my head in.' Max finally sits up properly and takes control of the wineglass and Amy relaxes. 'Mind if I skin up?' he says.

'What?'

'I could really do with rolling a joint right now, if you don't mind.'

Amy makes a good fist of hiding her surprise. 'Er, no, I guess not.' It seems everyone's up to it nowadays. 'I didn't know – ' she says rather pointlessly.

Max regards her reactions through half-closed eyes as he reaches into his pocket and takes out a pouch of rolling tobacco. 'You never smoked?'

'No. I mean, cigarettes, yes.'

Max's eyebrows go up. 'Really? I don't remember—'

'You wouldn't,' she says. 'I'm a bit of a secret smoker. And not very often.'

She watches him stick Rizlas together and lay out the papers and a line of tobacco before sprinkling in some strands of green vegetation and rolling it with surprising dexterity into a neat tube. He forms a strip of cardboard into a roach and pokes it into one end.

'Got an ashtray?' he says, twirling the spliff between his fingers.

'Oh, yes.'

She goes to the kitchen and gets it from under the sink. On the way back to the front room, she opens a drawer and takes out the pack of cigarettes that has been there untouched for days. When she returns, she puts her cigarettes down on the coffee table without taking one.

Max lights the spliff and blows on the flaming tip. The smell is immediate, burnt, pungent, a scent she recognises from the school grounds and quickly dispersing crowds of teenagers.

'Want some?'

'No, thanks. I'll stick to the fags.' She reaches one out of the pack and lights it self-consciously.

'I've told Karen,' says Max, leaning back into the sofa with the ashtray cradled in his lap so that she has to reach over him every time she wants to use it. 'Well, some of it. Not the what and the who, just that there's some trouble. That's your good influence at least.'

'Hey, don't blame me for anything,' she says, reflecting that she's the only one left around to blame for any of it. 'What's she say?'

'Oh, you know, the usual platitudes. They need to work through it for themselves, it'll all blow over in time – that kinda thing. You can't blame her: she doesn't know them, she doesn't know the situation. What could I expect her to say?'

'It'll be better when she's here,' says Amy.

'Sure you don't want any of this?' Max holds up the half-smoked joint, which she declines. She doesn't know what it'd do to her, and in a conversation like this, with Max drunk, she senses a need to keep her guard up. Even the normal cigarette is making her feel a little light-headed and she borrows the ashtray from Max's lap to grind it out, being careful about where she puts her hand.

'What the hell are we going to do?' Max says, sighing a cloud of dope smoke at her. It sounds rhetorical, until he starts adding some context. 'Have you spoken to your dad about it?'

The new 'it'.

'No,' she says, 'not yet. I daren't. What if I'm wrong? What if he doesn't know?'

'Well someone's got to tell him.'

'Do they? Like Karen says, maybe it'll all blow over.'

'Oh, not you as well.'

'We don't know how long it's been going on. It could be just a thing, something brought on by – the funeral and everything. We don't know how serious it is. What if they're just having a fling, recapturing lost youth or something? Or what if they're just talking about fucking horses?'

'In a hotel room in central London? I can think of better and cheaper places to get together to talk about fucking horses.'

'OK, admitted. But you know what I mean.'

'You're saying we shouldn't interfere.'

Amy thinks carefully about this. 'I'm saying not yet.'

'If not now, when?'

'I don't know. But I think we'll know when it's the right time. Don't you?'

'Not really. I don't think there'll ever be a right time. I think there'll be a crunch time when the shit hits the fan and the whole business is forced into the open. Then we'll have to do something.'

He takes a last drag of his spliff and screws it out in the ashtray. He's quiet for a long time, while Amy sips her wine. The next time she looks up he's fallen asleep. She switches on the TV, not bothered about disturbing him, which it doesn't. While she flips through the channels with the volume set low he begins gently snoring. The best thing is to let him sleep. She sits at the other end of the sofa and settles on a news programme.

Craig Sefton, shadow home secretary in the making, is being photographed on another podium speaking in front of a foreign-trade delegation. She watches with some interest, examining the camera-friendly face, trying to think if she's seen him before, possibly in the flesh, picturing him as somebody Colin might've introduced her to. She trawls through the memories of likely events and comes up with nothing. She's sure they've never met. The idea was just a fiction born out of her curiosity over Colin's journalistic interest in the man.

The item finishes and the news broadcast rolls on and then she's hearing the closing music; a reality game show follows, and soon the babble of the presenters has sent Amy to sleep as well.

When she wakes up the game show is over and Max is massaging her feet. She must have pulled her legs up onto the sofa while she was dozing. The foot rub was pleasant while she was floating in and out of wakefulness.

'Mmm.' The noise comes from her. Then one of the hands doing the rubbing begins to travel up her shin towards the back of her knee. The phrase EROGENOUS ZONE flashes in neon behind her eyelids and she quickly wakes to full alertness.

'Max.' The errant hand doesn't stop what it's doing. 'What are you doing?'

'Nothing,' says Max quietly. His voice has a dreamy satisfaction to it; he's clearly enjoying something. Amy draws her feet up, away from him, and his fingers cling indolently to one toe, reluctant to break the contact.

'Max, no. Feet yes, legs no. OK?'

'What?' he says, recommencing his massage but distinctly above the ankle.

'Please stop that.'

Max's hands let go of her feet and he shifts position on the settee, sliding his body in Amy's direction. She bolts to her feet and he collapses into the space she leaves behind.

'Oh,' he says, a bleat of disappointment.

'What's got into you?' she says, hoping to keep the situation light, fearing it'll take a lurch into seriousness.

'You have,' he says, sitting up and trying to look her square in the eyes. 'You know I like you.'

'Please, Max, this isn't right.'

'What? What's not right?' He's shuffling to his feet now, standing in front of her, swaying just a little, gripping her elbows as if to steady himself. She detects the dissemblance in it, but isn't ready to resort to extreme escape measures just yet. A perverse curiosity inside her wants to hear him out. 'You said it yourself. They're adults. They can do what they want. And so can we.'

'But I don't want,' Amy says. 'I don't even want to see you like this.' Her arms are squirming against the clasp of his hands now. 'What about Karen?'

'I know, we're getting married, for God's sake. So can't I have one last – adventure?'

The very idea and the way he chooses to express it nauseate her. She shakes his hands off her now and pushes him a step away from her.

'I think it's time you went now, please.' She's backing away, holding up her hands in the don't-touch-me gesture that she used with Winston. *If only Winston were here*, she thinks.

'Amy, come on.' He's walking forward, arms stretched out for a hug like Frankenstein's monster. 'Don't be like that.' She can tell he's not going to give up. Then suddenly he jumps back. 'Jesus!'

The noise from across the room almost makes her jump too even though she recognises it immediately: the ticking of claws on glass. Before Max has time to react further, she's crossing to the French windows, and Max is hanging back, too surprised at the sight of a wild animal up at the window to stop her.

'Is that a fox?' he asks as if she's never mentioned it to him before, except he clearly wasn't even listening.

'Course it's a fox,' says Amy using the key to unlock the door panels.

'Fuck's sake, don't let it in. What are you doing?'

Then they are open and the fox is actually coming inside, into the room. Max can only swear incomprehensibly as the animal springs towards him, takes up a firm-legged stance within a yard of where he is standing and sets up a repeated yap – part bark, part screech – that shatters the quiet of the room and bounces off the walls. Through all this Amy just stands and watches, her hand still on the handle of the French windows from having deliberately let the fucking thing inside. She glares across the room, not at the screaming fox but at him.

'Just leave, please, Max. Now.'

He can just hear her behind the noise. 'All right, all right. Fucking hell, this is insane.' He sidles away from the pissed-off animal towards the hall while the fox stands its ground, seeing him off. 'I need a taxi,' he pleads at Amy.

'It's North London – flag one down.'

Max doesn't argue, just moon-walks his way to the front door. The fox stands fast, it doesn't follow him into the hall, but he keeps looking back until he's outside and descending to the street, wondering what the hell just happened, wondering what the hell is going on.

Amy moves past the fox to the front door where she can see Max standing under a street light with his mouth wide open. She shuts the door and bolts it, already thinking the words *Good riddance*, and still it is quite some time before the significance of the phrase dawns on her.

38

Can we talk – please?

When Amy walks into the school library Winston makes a point of keeping his head down and continues to scribble at the notes he's making on *Othello*. This proves to no avail when she comes over and sits down opposite him at the same table. Thankfully, no one else is sitting at it because she takes out a piece of paper and pencils this note and pushes it across at him. He takes the note and writes something beneath her question and passes it back to her.

You picked the wrong place.

He sees her smile and his feelings towards her thaw a degree or two. He packs his stuff away into his hold-all and stands up and heads for the door. Amy doesn't wait but immediately follows him outside. Winston says nothing, not even trying to guess what she could want.

Perhaps remembering the last time they had anything resembling a conversation, Amy is appropriately sheepish. 'I think I owe you an apology.'

'For what?'

She has no ready answer. After a moment she says, 'I treated you badly.'

'You had your reasons,' he says. Like her mother's *I don't know what you want me to say*, Winston's reply engages with the emotional truth through the statement of a bald fact, but it rings less vacuous to her.

'Can we meet to talk? Not in school. Somewhere else.'

He doesn't need long to think about it. 'OK. Where?'

'I don't know. What about that pub?'

'What, the Wetherspoon's?'

'Is that OK?'

'When?'

'What are you doing tonight?'

'What d'you think I'm doing? Exactly what I'm doing now. It's two weeks to the exams, Miss.'

'Yes, I'm sorry. I wasn't thinking. Forget it.'

He lets her stew in her guilt for a moment before saying, 'It's a'ight. Tonight's cool. I can give you an hour.'

'When? You decide.'

'Eight?'

'OK. See you there?' She starts to turn away then stops. 'Thanks, Winston.'

As she walks off down the hall Winston doesn't know whether to feel angry, anxious or happy. He suspects what he is actually feeling is a mixture of all three.

39

'Thanks for meeting me. I really appreciate it.'

The pub is busy and humming with a healthy early-evening crowd of drinkers. She gets there in good time so that she can save them a table, and is sitting waiting for him with a Diet Coke when he arrives. She's taken the liberty of buying him a J2O so that he won't have to wait at the bar. They aren't exactly overstaffed. He sits down and crosses one leg over the other loosely, one ankle pivoting on the opposite knee, his long legs creating a distance between them.

'Just say what you've got to say,' he says, clutching his bottle.

'I'm not sure what I want to say. There's been some shit going on in my life and I wished you'd been there to talk to.'

That's blunt. It makes a favourable impression on Winston, but then he knows that's what she's trying to do. He needs to be careful how he responds.

'You're not the only one. Welcome to planet Earth.'

She gives a pitiable little laugh, the wordless equivalent of a *Touché!* At least she isn't coming across as the middle-class, better-than-thou witch he was afraid she'd turned out to be. He knows she'd be pleased he thinks *witch* instead of *bitch* now, but he keeps his mouth shut about it.

'It's been a bad week,' Amy says, 'and I found myself wishing I had someone there to talk about it with. And it was you.'

Winston is touched but he still doesn't want to show it. His defence mechanisms make him lift up and take a swig from his drink and he feels conscious that it unintentionally signals his discomfort. This whole situation is so far outside his comfort zone.

'Did you see the fox again?' He poses the question in a way carefully intended not to seem like he's taking the piss. Whatever he feels towards her, he has no desire to be cruel.

'Yeah, I did actually.'

Did it talk? a part of him wants to ask, though he stays silent.

'I – think I know now what it might've said to me that

night I was telling you about,' says Amy.

'Yeah?'

'Yeah. I think it was warning me.'

'About what?'

'Who to trust; who not to trust. Do you trust foxes?'

Now it's Winston's turn to laugh, not with pathos but with genuine amusement. 'That has got to be one of the weirdest questions I've ever been asked seriously.'

'I bet farmers get asked it all the time,' Amy says off the cuff.

Winston reaches inside his pocket and pulls out his mobile or BlackBerry or whatever it is. Amy waits a moment while he taps at the keys with some obvious purpose. 'Here we go,' he says at last, finding what he was looking for on the gadget. '"Madam, 'tis true; and were't not madness then, to make the fox surveyor of the fold?"' He looks up at her from the screen. '*Henry VI, Part Two*, apparently.'

'Have you read it?' she says.

'Not recently.'

Don't bother,' she says. 'Not till after your exams anyway. How's the revision going?'

'Music's a doddle. The rest of it isn't.'

'Well that's honest. If there's anything I can help you with . . . '

'That goes without saying. You're a good teacher, Miss.'

She smiles. 'Amy.'

He only needs to look at her without saying anything.

'Does that make any sense' – he looks down at the screen again – '". . . were't not madness then, to make the fox surveyor of the fold?"?'

Amy thinks about it for a moment. 'Depends who the fox is.'

'It'd mean something to me if it made some sense. I told you how much it frightens me – this premonition thing.' She notices his use of the term that she suggested, before thinking suddenly that Roz Lincoln might've got there first. It doesn't matter. 'I wish I can find some way to control it. That's what's frightening about it. If I felt I could control it then I could start to live with it. You know what I mean?'

'I do know what you mean,' she says. 'But you've got to

179

face the fact that you can't control it. Not if it's something outside yourself, outside ordinary human experience.' She's aware of skating on thin ice; she doesn't want to bring up the old hoodoo voodoo upset, labelling him a freak, so she presses on. 'If it's something inside, that's a different matter. You have to decide. Is it a special gift, talent, whatever, or is it all in your mind? Are you just crazy? And it doesn't even have to be outside the bounds of ordinary human experience. I think we all face that question in our lives all the time, whoever or whatever we are or think we are. Am I different from everyone else or am I just crazy? If you can answer that question that's the first step towards some kind of accommodation with it, and that's all the control you can hope for.'

Winston ponders for a moment. 'You know who that reminds me of? Winston Smith, *Nineteen Eighty-four*.'

Amy feels a thrill course through her body. 'You read it?'

'Well, don't sound too surprised, it's not that long. Two hundred and fifty pages or somefing.' She reaches out and pats her hand down on his thigh. She doesn't mean anything by it other than a gesture of genuine teacherly pride and he doesn't try to make anything out of it. 'Listen, I'm sorry but I really gotta go,' he says. 'When I said I could spare an hour I was exaggerating that. It's not that I haven't had a great time or nothing, I'm just really busy at the moment.'

'The revision,' she provides instinctively; she isn't thinking: she doesn't want it to sound like a test, provoking reactions she might be able to read in him.

'You know,' he says passing it over, 'I still don't know what it is you wanted to see me about.'

Before she can stop herself she reaches across and squeezes his hand and Roz Lincoln outside a bookmaker's shop front flashes through her brain. But that's something she will keep to herself, something for another time, if ever.

'It can wait,' says Amy. 'I just wanted to see you.'

'Thanks,' says Winston.

'For what?'

'For not bringing up the – the thing we were discussing last time we talked like this.'

'I was a bit of a cow, wasn't I?'

'Like I say, you have your reasons.'

'It's my job. You understand?'

'Yeah, course it's your job, innit? I'm not disputin' that an' I respect your position. And you know I would never breathe a word about us to anyone.'

She feels herself go red at his use of the 'us' word. Images of their night of sex together race through her mind. And here he is sitting next to her in a pub now – again. The old what-am-I-doing question rears its tired head in the distance but she is learning to ignore its puny roar.

'I know. Besides, you're eighteen, you're an adult, you can do what you want. Except,' she adds, quickly, 'it's illegal of course. But I mean apart from that – '

'You're not tryin' to wind me up, are you?'

She forces herself to look serious. 'Like I said, there's been some shit going on in my life but I don't see why I should take it out on you. You're a good person.'

It's Winston this time who reaches out and squeezes Amy's hand.

'I'm glad we're friends again. It's been fuckin' awful in school. I've been dreadin' being alone with you. I wish we could be alone now though.'

Amy picks up the hand she was holding and places it firmly but gently back in his lap. 'Just friends,' she says. 'You've got your exams coming up. So just friends. For now.'

Winston looks like he can live with that.

40

The night Max came round drunk and stoned was the last Amy saw of the fox and she doesn't discuss the details of the event with anyone, not even Winston. Not that she isn't tempted, it's just that the poor boy has enough on his plate without her unloading her troubles on him as well right now.

In retrospect she harbours no ill will towards Max. Her level of respect for him may have gone down a notch or two, but she recognises that he is in a bad place emotionally at the moment. When she recalls him backing out of the house in something approaching fear of the wild, baying animal, she sees it as something rather pathetic and she feels a little sorry for him and for the way things have gone between them. She honestly hopes and believes that they can get over it without any of the protracted, predictable episodes of gender polarisation and injured pride.

In the meantime she continues to tell herself that the fox is Colin, or that at least some ineffable relationship exists between the fox and her deceased husband. She doesn't know what to think about the soul or universal consciousness beyond the contemporary rationalist saw that such things are no more than dreams, delusions and wishful thinking. All she knows is that the fox came to her defence when it perceived her to be under threat. At least that's what appeared to happen. Or is she making the old mistake of personifying it again, attributing human qualities to it when it may simply have sensed a presence it regarded as a threat to itself? No, that answer just won't fit the bill. A fox scenting danger will turn and run, not put up an aggressive front, unless it's cornered or surrounded – or unless it's young are being threatened, or something or someone that is equally important to it. But why would any old fox choose to protect her, or any human being? None of it makes any sense in a world predicated entirely on reason and enlightenment.

Amy continues to hold off from taking up the offer in her mother's text, or indeed from contacting her mother at all. She doesn't feel ready for that conversation yet. She's worried about her father though. If this thing is tearing the Trent household apart, what is it doing to her own father? She has to know, and contrives to visit him at home one morning while her mother is unspecifiably elsewhere.

'Where is she, do you know?' she asks him as pointedly as she dare.

'I don't keep track of your mother's comings and goings anymore,' he says, settling his daughter in the same huge armchair that would swallow her up as a child, and which she used to love to sit in with a picture book in her lap. Somewhere, the little girl turned a corner and emerged as the troubled young widow before him today, and it breaks his heart to see it.

'You mean you don't know where she is or what she's doing?'

'I'm sure she told me but I have trouble listening to something I've heard more than a dozen times before. Telling someone about your routine is as uninteresting to me as telling someone what you dreamt last night. If it doesn't create a memorable narrative I'm afraid the details are going to slip out of my head and I'm not going to care very much.'

These are harsh words coming from her father, and she isn't going to let them past without a challenge. 'You mean in one ear, out the other?'

He declines to rise to the bait. 'Something like that, yes.' He fiddles self-consciously with the temples of his glasses, trying to lace them with his restless fingers.

'How long has it been like this, Dad? I mean between you and Mum.'

'Like what? You make it sound like a tragedy.' He spreads his arms to display the collected material wealth of two full adult lives around him. 'Do I look like I'm sitting in the middle of a tragedy?'

The literary definition of tragedy to which he is alluding doesn't escape her: not the tragedy of a road smash, a bomb in Iraq or a bungee-jumping accident but the tragedy of a hero's downfall, triggered – locked into fate – by a flaw in his or her own character. The irony is that the circumstances of her father's life indicated by his open-armed gesture at the room, the house, the property, the family photographs, is of the road-accident variety; and the tragedy that he is denying is the making of his own – reasonableness. There's his flaw, she realises now. It's something that she always regarded as a strength, a positive, which is now letting her down: his willingness to live and let live, to take what comes and muddle through, not pretending it isn't happening but just letting it be. Things will always turn out for the best one way or another. That's his tragedy, and for the first time in her life Amy can see nothing heroic in it.

'Do you do anything together? Do you – I don't know – have any kind of a life together?'

'Your mother and I have always had different interests. For a while she was interested in my interests – music, theatre, the life of the mind. I know – bit of a grandiose phrase, but I don't mind admitting I like it. She used to say that's what first attracted her to me. I was an intellectual, and in the world she came from there were no intellectuals. Culture was something you bought by the yard, like library books. You had a man make it up for you, you didn't labour at it yourself. Trouble is, after a while I think she began to appreciate more why you don't labour at it yourself – because that kind of work takes patience and commitment, two things your mother's never properly understood. Patience and commitment to herself, to her own interests, yes, she's got that in spades. But patience and commitment to an idea, to a value – I just don't think she ever really had the guts for that.' He pauses; she can almost see him reaching for the pipe he used to smoke and gave up years ago. 'But do we have a life together? I'd say we do. I'd say we've got two: you and Alice. That's what counts.'

Amy is getting angry with him now. He's at once too detached and too understanding. Either that or he's ducking the issue. She feels herself coming to a stage in a road beyond which she can travel no farther. Must she spell the situation out to him? She knows he understands what's going on; one of them needs to drag it out into the open and she can see it isn't going to be him.

'Doesn't it worry you not knowing where she is? Not knowing who she's with?'

'Is that what this is about? Is that why you came to see me? If so, you can put it out of your mind. I appreciate the concern, sweetheart, but it's mine and your mother's business, no one else's.'

Amy knows she has no right to push it any further. He's only adopting the same stance that she herself adopts when her parents try to interfere in her affairs. But this isn't just about the three of them – or four if you set Alice a place at the table. It *is* her business because she's the link, the focal point of two families coming together in an unholy union.

'But Dad, it's Colin's father.' She braves herself to watch his face and it doesn't change. 'It's Edward, for God's sake. You do know that, don't you?'

Then his face alters; it morphs into something she hasn't seen before, doesn't even remember from childhood. The palimpsest of sadness is no longer visible beneath; there's only irritation, verging on anger.

'How do you know all this?' He pierces her with a desperate stare, and for a second she feels like a chastened little girl before him again.

'From Max. He's been updating me on his parents.'

The enflamed emotion cools in her father's face and it sinks back into a more contemplative, sympathetic and normal state of rest. He is quiet for a very long time, not looking at her, staring at a point in space, or perhaps at a picture reel in front of his mind's eye. Eventually, after evidently weighing his words – since he uses them so sparingly – he speaks.

'If it wasn't him it would be someone else. I'm sorry for Christine, I'm sure she doesn't deserve it. But that's between her and Edward.'

'So you're giving in. Is that what you're saying?'

'What I'm saying is that what's between them is between them. And what's between your mother and me is – I'm afraid – very little and fast dwindling to nothing at all. But that's OK. I've got enough in my life to keep me going.'

She thinks of his books, his piano, his water colours, his various retirement projects. She thinks of her mother's comment about getting him out of his study. What the hell do men do in studies? Surround themselves with unread encyclopædias; enslave themselves to a computer screen; make themselves a little den where like small boys they can hide from their family and the world. When you're a child that's OK, it's your den, it's a giggle. When you're her father's age it's no longer a giggle; it's a panic room, a bunker, a tomb.

'Dad, what are you going to do?' she asks hopelessly.

'Just leave it, love. These things have a way of sorting themselves out. You'll see.'

185

More platitudes. Funny how platitudes have a habit of putting an end to a conversation. She experiences a tug of compunction to ask him if it's all right to talk to Mum about it, until it strikes her that it would apparently mean nothing to him whether she does or doesn't.

'If you need me, anytime – ' she says as she's leaving.

'Even before midday on a Saturday?'

'Even before midday on a Saturday.'

41

Amy comes away from her visit to her dad feeling pleasantly upbeat. Little in the way of a practical solution has come of it but that isn't what she went there for. Anyway, how can you have a solution to something that's not so much a problem as a situation? Amy has never approved of collocating 'solve' with 'a situation' – something she drums out of her students if they ever do it. And that's what this is: a situation that they all have to deal with. What she really went there for, she now recognises, is to be a part of the situation. It feeds her growing sense of moving on with her life, being involved with other people. She knows there's a bit of self-aggrandisement in there, but knowing that she showed support for her father is the most important element.

Amy leaves it a couple of days before contacting her mother. Perhaps a part of her makes her wait until the weekend just to see what will happen. If that's the case it seems to score a result.

She gets her on her mobile.

'My God, will wonders never cease? You calling me before midday on a Saturday?'

The apposite sarcasm makes Amy wonder if her father has said anything to her mother about her visit; he indicated that he didn't intend to but she is too damn good at weasling things like that out of him.

'I got your text,' says Amy. 'Still want a chat?'

'Today? Oh no, I'm sorry, darling, that's out of the question.'

'What are you doing? Gardening?'

'No, dear, I'm not gardening, I've got a meeting.'

'What kind of meeting?'

'What do you mean, what kind of meeting? A *meeting* meeting.' She becomes impatient with Amy's silence. 'A race meeting.'

'I thought it was show jumping you were into.' She knows the indication of a lack of interest in her hobbies will needle her.

'You know, Amy, "into" used like that is so vulgar.'

'I didn't know you went to the races.'

'You know me, darling: where there's a horse . . .'

She's making the horse thing into a cloak to hide behind, and Amy realises that for all she knows she could've been doing that all her life.

'Where is it?'

'Where's what, dear?'

'This horse race.' She picks the baldest term she can think of and it's still nowhere near bald enough.

'Sandown Park. Why, are you coming?'

'Would you want me to be there?'

'Well I wouldn't have thought it was quite up your street. You never took an interest in horses. Not like Alice. At least she showed keen for a few years.'

'Which is all very well, Mother, but it doesn't answer the question. Would you want me to be there?'

'Well whyever wouldn't I?'

Amy suspects she's calling her bluff.

'Where can I find you and who do I ask for?'

'Oh, come now, Amy, you don't actually want to attend a race meeting. You know you'll be bored to tears and the rest of us will have to bear the brunt of it.'

Amy doesn't miss the use of the 'us' word, but then of course she's bound to be with somebody. Mother is not the type to go anywhere alone: that too would be vulgar. 'Where will you be?'

'Can't this wait until tomorrow?'

Amy steels her resolve. 'No. I'm coming.'

'Very well. We'll be in the Lanson bar.'

'And how do I get in?'

'You'll need a ticket or an invitation.'

'Yes, Mother. I presume you're going as a non-paying guest of somebody or other. So how do I freeload my way in?'

'Oh, I don't know. There are a number of patrons. Say you're a guest of Craig Sefton. I'll get his people to put you on the list. If there's a problem, ring this number. Amy. Amy. Are you still there?'

Amy nearly dropped the phone but is still hanging onto it, barely listening. She brings herself to focus. 'Yes, I'm here.'

'OK. But don't dawdle. The first race is at two. And wear something nice, not trousers. Here's the number. It's – '

Later Amy finds she actually managed to write the number down in her notebook, though after the unnerving shock of hearing Sefton's name on her mother's lips, she has no recollection of actually putting it there.

42

Amy changes out of her weekend clothes into her all-purpose little black dress which she last wore to Colin's funeral, then looks up how to get to Sandown Park. She takes a Tube train south of the river to Waterloo then boards an overland train to Esher and is there in not much more than an hour.

It's the first time Amy has been to the horse races since her student days, when she went once under peer pressure and distinctly failed to enjoy it. She's never been to the Sandown Park racecourse, but once inside the grounds it doesn't take her long to locate the Lanson bar. She gets let in, no trouble, but the skin at the back of her neck tingles when she drops Craig Sefton's name to the man on the door, as it did at the main entrance.

Where she was expecting to see her mother inspecting fetlocks in a paddock, she finds her instead in an atmosphere of fine dining and expensive champagne cocktails. No wonder she likes to move with the horsy set. Amy feels suddenly privy to a side of her mother's life she knew of but never knew the nature of; rather than feeling privileged though, she feels a witness to something sordid, something that was never meant for her. Perhaps coming here today was a rash mistake but there is nothing she can do about that now.

'Pull up a pew, dear,' her mother says, sitting at a table already littered with culinary delights, among a group of people that she doesn't introduce to Amy and who ignore her arrival, their eyes glued to the view of the home straight up to the finishing post and the heads of the busy punters in the enclosure beneath the grandstand that they have from the picture window. Amy slides up a chair and sits down. While her mother is occupied peering through a pocket-sized pair of binoculars she cranes her head round at the people in the bar. Consciously, she's looking for her father-in-law, and unconsciously she's looking for the politician whose name she keeps encountering and whose face she keeps seeing on TV. At the moment she can see neither of them.

'If you're looking for the runners, they're here,' says her mother handing Amy a copy of that day's race card. Amy glances at it, not taking in any of the information, more simply acknowledging that an object of some description has been thrust into her hands.

'I didn't expect to find you here on your own,' she says, finding her voice at last.

'I'm not, silly.'

'Amy!'

It's Edward's voice behind her. She swivels round on her chair and there he is bending over her for a kiss. She responds automatically as though nothing is out of place, not knowing what she is doing.

'Your mother said you were coming. This is rather a turn-up for the books, isn't it? Let me get you a glass, you can help us with the champagne. Have you eaten yet?'

'I'm not hungry,' she manages to say as his attention drifts, searching for a waiter. There is an exchange of words and signals and a liveried youth goes off to do Edward's bidding. While his back is turned to them, Amy shoots a look at her mother which she intends to be read as disapproving, and her mother predictably ignores it, refusing to be disapproved of.

'Picked any likely winners yet?' says Edward, standing behind them and leaning over to pour champagne into the glass that the waiter has fetched. Amy isn't sure if he's talking to her or her mother or both of them.

'I rather fancy Look What You've Done in the two-thirty,' her mother replies. 'Fabulous form all season and very good at this distance, though I'm a little worried the going might be too firm. It hasn't rained here, has it?'

'Not that I'm aware of,' says Edward, 'but they'll have watered. How about you, Amy? Fancy anything in the two o'clock?'

Amy was only vaguely aware of the time now, her head spinning somewhat with the absurdity of the situation she's put herself in. She slowly realises he's talking about the first race.

'I've – got no idea,' she says instinctively, taking the drink that he's lifted up and is holding out to her. Yes; a drink. That's what she feels she needs. She sips it and stands it on the table and pretends to read the race card her mother has given her. When the words stop swimming in front of her eyes, she finds the list of runners in the two o'clock.

Why do they give race horses such ludicrous names? It's a thought that has struck her before in idle moments when racing's been in the background on the telly. It surprises her that anyone is able to remember the names of horses from one race to the next. In fact, she can't recall a single instance of her knowingly hearing the same name twice. She lets her eyes trail down the card until one of them stands out.

'Spotted something?' says Edward.

'Oh, just – ' She feels foolish; she doesn't know how one goes about this sort of thing, not to mention that she's reluctant to take part anyway.

'Go on,' he insists.

'Well, that one,' she says, pointing stupidly at a name she could just as easily have read out loud.

'Let's have a look,' he says, taking the card from her. 'Cherie Amour. It's got a good starting price.'

'But what do I know?' Amy says feebly.

'Well let's find out, shall we? Let me put a bet on it for you.'

'No!' She surprises herself with the force of her own voice. 'Don't be silly.' Now she's using their lingo, her mother's lingo, and her mind recalls the time she and Max made fun of the word. It seems ages ago, much longer ago than the funeral, which she knows isn't possible.

'Nonsense,' says Edward. 'It's come to something if I can't stand my own daughter-in-law a flutter on the gee-gees.'

Why are they all talking as though they're in kindergarten, she wonders.

'I – don't know what to do,' she says. 'I've never put a bet on.'

'No trouble,' he says. 'Easy as pie. We don't even have to leave the bar. Back in a mo.'

He disappears off somewhere and Amy turns to her mother.

'Mother, what are you doing here?'

'I beg your pardon?'

'What are you doing here with Edward? With Colin's dad.'

'Now what kind of a question is that?' her mother replies. 'And how would you like me to answer it? Naïvely?

192

Disingenuously? I've no wish to hide anything from you, you know, so there's no need for you to put on the hard-done-by routine.'

'I'm not— '

'Edward and I happen to have a great deal in common. We have had for a long time. And time is something that we've both found is moving on, so there's no sense in wasting it.'

Amy doesn't know what to say. It seems that her mother has said it all while actually saying very little.

'I'm not thinking of me,' says Amy, about to supply the names of the people she would claim to be thinking of.

'Good,' her mother interrupts, 'because neither am I.' She pauses, probing for once the hurt her comment may have caused. 'I'm sorry to be so blunt, dear, but that's just how it is, I'm afraid. I can't see the need to play games any longer. Speaking of which, you wouldn't know anything about an empty note, will you?'

Amy feels defeated. If she shows that she does, the tables will be turned on her because she will've become the player of games. If she pretends she doesn't know what her mother is talking about, then her mother will let the remark disperse in a cloud of obfuscation.

'There we go, all done.' Edward is back. He hands Amy a betting slip: Cherie Amour in the two o'clock, a hundred pounds placed, ten to one to win. Her mind is still reeling too much from the conversation with her mother for her to take it in properly. She becomes aware that the race is about to start. Everyone is looking, Amy isn't sure where until her eyes find the line of horses dancing and whinnying with anticipation under their jockeys at the starting gate. Before she knows what's happening they're off, all moving together at the sound of some signal she never heard, and the collective voice of the crowd below and the people around her in the bar grind up like a hurdy-gurdy, spurring them on.

'We don't have anything on this one, do we?' It's her mother asking Edward. How very like her to ignore Amy's bet, to deny her the likelihood of any excitement, to think only of herself and her own interests.

Amy continues looking out of the window, though she can no longer see any of the runners except perhaps one still bringing up the rear in the direction that the others have vanished. The noise in the bar grows in intensity and she wonders what they're all still cheering or cursing at, until she sees the downward-angled TV monitors high above the window.

'Come on,' says Edward behind her.

'I thought we had nothing on this one,' her mother persists.

'It's Amy's,' says Edward. 'Damn thing's romping home.' Amy feels his hand descend onto her shoulder. 'Well spotted, old love.'

Amy feels a thrill of excitement at the news, immediately hating herself for it but craning her neck to look up at the screen. 'Where? Which one is it?'

'It's there,' says Edward, his hand getting animated on her shoulder, giving it an encouraging, companionable squeeze. Amy thinks she oughtn't to like it but she's getting caught up in the thrill now, and her feelings are mashed to a pudding. 'Right out in front. The favourite's on his tail but he's holding his ground.'

She hasn't heard a racket like this since the last time she watched a football match with Colin in a pub. The bar was an uproar of threats, hollers and imprecations, the uncouth voices both male and female.

'Here they come, look. Go on,' yells Edward. Amy is still looking at the TV screen until she realises everyone else is looking at the panorama out of the window where the front-runners can now be seen flying down the home straight. Then, as abruptly as it started up, the noise is wheezing down again, the race over, the result obviously undisputed. 'You did it, by God. You backed a winner.'

Amy finds herself lifted out of her seat and all of a sudden Edward's arms are around her and he's hugging her tightly.

'Did I?' she says, confused about what just happened and what is supposed to happen now.

'Yes, you bloody well did!' He separates from the hug, still holding her by the arms very much in the way his only surviving son held onto her just a couple of nights ago, but without the sense of drunken menace. 'I say, where's that betting slip?'

She offers it to him, able to see how excited he is.

'Do you mind?' he says. 'Come with me if you like.'

'Where?'

'To collect your winnings, of course.'

'Oh,' says Amy, dithering. Does she want to go gallivanting off with him or stay here with her mother? Neither prospect particularly pleases her. 'You go,' she says. 'It was your bet really.'

'Nonsense. Back in a minute.'

She sits back down and takes a sip of the champagne, noticing it's gone warm as if from all the energy given off in the room during the commotion of the race.

'Clever girl,' she hears her mother say. 'Cherie Amour. Anyone I know?'

Amy ignores the remark. She ignores her mother altogether until Edward returns.

'There you are,' he says, proffering a bundle of bank notes.

'I can't, Edward. It was your bet. I didn't risk anything.'

'Now come on. You said you'd let me put a bet on for you. You can't go backing out now it's all come up roses. I've got my stake back. The rest is yours.'

Amy takes the money and starts counting it without thinking. 'God,' she says, 'how much is here?'

'A thousand pounds, of course.'

'Edward, this is too much,' she says, though she knows it's too late now, knows that she will have to accept it. She doesn't like it and she isn't even really sure why, but she knows that she will have to accept it all.

She's said all she came to say. Actually, she's said nothing that she came to say. All that's happened is that she's discovered she has nothing to say, or rather that she is in fact powerless to say anything. In the face of what's happening here, what is there for her to say?

As she's turning to leave a stranger approaches her. It takes her only a second to recognise him as the face from television that seems to have been haunting her in recent weeks.

'You're Marian's daughter,' he says, holding his hand out to her. She shakes it, her face suddenly burning, her brain nagging her with the futile message, *It's him, it's him.* 'I'm Craig

Sefton.'

He looks younger than on TV, the smile wider, the hairline lower and the brow less creased.

'Oh. Hi. Amy Trent.'

'I thought so,' he says. 'I hope you don't mind. I know David attended your husband's funeral.'

'David?' she hears herself asking.

'Cameron.'

'Oh yes,' she says, thinking, *It wasn't the funeral, it was the wake*, but leaving it be.

'I just wanted to say that I'm sorry for your loss.' *Sorry for your loss*. TV dialogue, she reflects, is there no getting away from it? Until he adds, 'I lost someone special myself recently. My thoughts and prayers go out to you.'

She looks him steadily in the eye for the first time since he came up to her, realising suddenly that he isn't making a campaign pitch, that behind the public façade, somewhere in there is a genuine human being.

'Thank you,' she says.

43

Amy dreams that night about the fox killer. She knows this is most definitely a dream even as she is having it because in it she possesses a Japanese samurai sword which Colin used years ago in his kendo practice. Except that there is no such sword and there never has been. The club he was a member of only ever practised with bamboo staves, Colin never owned such a weapon and to do so, even to attempt to bring one into the country, would've been illegal. Even as she is dreaming, she's aware of all these contingencies so that she feels fully in control and immune from any harm that the fox killer could do to her. Nonetheless, the sword feels palpable and its pristine steel is cool, real and empowering to her touch.

He doesn't look like Bob from *Twin Peaks*, he looks like plain old Bob Revill, the man in the woolly hat and spectacles who knocked on her door and spoke to her frankly but politely only a week or so ago. This time though he's carrying his gun with him. It's a long-barrelled firearm, some kind of rifle or maybe a shotgun, she isn't sure which, and the two of them are in the road outside her house standing facing each other a short distance apart in what is evidently a showdown.

Bob Revill puts the butt of the gun to his shoulder to take aim at her but it is all done in laughably slow motion so that she has what feels like an eternity to lift the blade over her head in a two-handed grip that she remembers from a hundred violent movies. While Bob is still raising his weapon Amy is charging towards him, positioning her physique for the delivery of a devastating double blow. She reaches him before the gun goes off, which it never does. Before it can be discharged Amy has swung the blade in a downward arc, cutting through metal and slicing the barrel clean off. In the same motion, on the cusp of the parabola, she turns the sword deftly in her hand for the upswing. The steel edge bites into Bob's body at his left hip and doesn't stop until it reaches his right shoulder, cutting him diagonally almost completely in two.

Amy wakes up. The memory of the sword strike is still vivid, but a part of her mind feels exhausted, as if from grappling all night with a difficult question. By whatever process it has been achieved the answer has come to her. She will give the money to Winston. It may not be much in this day and age and it will probably represent little incentive to give up his dope dealing; hopefully, she'll be able to convince him of her good intentions without attaching any strings to the gift. Once it's his he can do what he wants with it – keep it as a nest egg, spend it on equipment for the band or take a well-earned holiday after his exams are over.

Her mind keeps returning to his predictions, the string of expressions coined by Shakespeare that he quoted at her. She accepts now that, for these at least, predictions was the appropriate word. She sees however that the order was wrong, or at best misleading.

To thine own self be true. That part chimes with her decision about the win from the race track. She doesn't want Edward's money, she couldn't take it and still look at herself in the mirror every day, but she's be happy for someone else to put it to good use. *A sorry sight.* Well that one works on a number of levels. The sight of Max drunk the other night when he was trying to paw at her and making a fool of himself. What she herself must've looked like – what she would have looked like if she'd been able to see herself – waking up shameless and hung over in Winston's bed that Sunday morning. And on another level, one that is yet to occur, what she expects poor Christine to look like the next time they meet.

The incident with Max and his ejection from her house by the fox takes care of the *Good riddance* part.

The only bit left that she can't make any emotional sense of is the stuff about truth. *The truth will out, the naked truth.*

Ever since the accident Amy has felt that she's striving towards some kind of truth about something. No, be honest. She's been striving towards some kind of truth about herself. Isn't that why she isolated herself so successfully from other people, people that she loves, so that she completely failed to notice that their world was crumbling apart in a way she could never have imagined? She's been obsessed with the pursuit of her own truths to such a degree that she put her career in jeopardy and her family out of mind.

And what has she discovered in the process? Nothing. Except that there is still one truth to be uncovered. All this time she's been trying to look for something inside herself and after all this time the search, quest, whatever, has left her little more satisfied than she was at the start. She realises now that she's been looking in the wrong place all along. This isn't about her. It's about Colin. The one truth still to be uncovered.

The thing beneath Max's jacket: the thing on the tape.

44

'Thank you for coming,' she says.

Max hovers on the doorstep, wondering if that constitutes an invitation to step inside. After his last visit he knows how carefully he has to tread to make things up to her. After a moment or two during which he inspects the stoop and various other features around the front entrance in an effort to avoid eye contact, she tells him to come in.

'Do you want a drink?' she asks him as he stands in the kitchen not daring to even sit without an invitation.

'I'd have thought after last time—' he begins, but she doesn't let him go any further.

'Forget last time,' she says. 'We both made mistakes.'

'Did we? What was yours?'

'I let you in.'

'Oh yeah. Right.'

'This time I've invited you in. No need for apologies. Let's forget it happened.'

'If you can, I will,' he says. 'But I'm still sorry. I shouldn't have—'

'Like I said, forget it. What's done is done. Time to move on. I don't want it to come between us for good.'

'No.' A negative charge of satisfaction passes between them.

'Did you bring it?' The question is a formality: she's already looking down at what's in his hand. He holds it up.

'Are you sure about this?' he says.

'I want to see it.'

'I can tell you what's on it, you know. You don't have to watch it.'

'Don't,' she says. 'Don't tell me. Just show me.'

'Are you absolutely sure?'

'We went through all this on the phone. For the last time, yes.'

They go through to the front room and Max hands the video cassette over to Amy. It's ages since she last had an occasion to use the VCR but she's already spent a frustrating half hour working it all out and connecting the right cables to the right sockets before Max arrived. If all is as she trusts it is, it should work. She hopes it won't let her down. She'd hate to appear incompetent in front of him at this stage.

'I just—'

'Don't,' she says, pushing in the cassette and getting ready with the remote. 'Just – don't, all right?'

Max keeps his mouth shut as the tape starts rolling and the lead-in fuzz turns to a blank, stable darkness, turning into the opening captions and credits.

CCTV SEX – 100% FROM REAL CCTV CAMERA FOOTAGE, are the first words that appear on the screen.

Amy gives a sneering little laugh. 'Do we really need the word "from" there?'

Before Max can say anything they're into CHANGING ROOM QUICKIE and the boy's shirt-tailed arse moving in and out between the legs of his camera-oblivious girlfriend. While Max dips his head, only half-looking at the blurry image on the screen, he hears Amy start to chuckle quietly.

'Is this it?' she asks. 'Is this really what I've been losing so much sleep over?'

She can tell from Max's silence that it isn't.

'May I?' he says, holding out his hand towards her.

Amy passes him the remote control and he presses the fast forward button with the picture still running. A blur of half-obscured head-nodding and bare-arsed disco dancing cavorts in front of her eyes until he presses the PLAY button again and the image settles on a spot past a new caption that she just missed. Some cheesy music tinkles over the moving pictures. Max hands her back the remote and she returns her attention to the screen.

It's hard to tell at first if the image is in black and white or colour. A single static camera shot from high above, presumably in the corner of a ceiling, has captured someone in a room. The room looks like a large dining room, by which she takes it to be a dining hall, like the function room of a big hotel. The light is dim, as though the room has been shut off, and clearly it's evening, but she can make out the man standing at the end of a long table, possibly a row of tables, arrayed behind him and stretching away beyond the far boundary of the camera's image. The man seems to be smartly dressed but something about him looks dated. She notices he's wearing a narrow, old-fashioned tie like the one Max had wore to Colin's funeral. Like the one he wore to their wedding. She notices, in fact, with a sudden tweak of her brain, that the man in the image *is* Max.

Amy looks across her own front room at the real Max who is sitting here with her now and he notices her glance because he's only half-looking at the screen himself, and he wordlessly signals to her that it's OK, that she should keep watching – that it's too late for anything else.

As her eyes return to the screen, a second figure emerges from downstage, as it were, into the frame. Amy can't see for certain who she is because her back remains to the camera, which never captures her face, but it's a woman – and this is where the image puzzles Amy as to whether it's truly in monochrome because she knows somehow that the sleeveless dress the woman is wearing is emerald green, not any other colour that the grainy image could possibly have represented, but a vivid emerald green. She knows it because the dress the woman is wearing is the same dress that she herself wore to the party on her own wedding night, the night of her own wedding reception at the Devonshire Arms, deep in the Buckinghamshire countryside.

She remembers the room now; a room that had played host to another function earlier that same afternoon but on the night in question was shut off in darkness, not part of their wedding reception, technically off limits, but somehow left accessible. The tables, shadowy in the background, had been cleared of their detritus but the room had remained unlocked, secreted away and discovered, she remembers now, by just the two of them – first Max, then her: the blushing bride, all set for her honeymoon night in a plush suite upstairs somewhere with her currently otherwise engaged new husband, and her fresh-out-of-the-bag brother-in-law, mysterious, barely known to her, newly returned from some impressively exotic adventure in a far-off land, back in England for the happy occasion.

The two figures in the image seem to converse with one another, but not for long. Presently, the woman puts a finger up to the man's lips, deliberately silencing whatever protest has risen to them, before bending her knees and crouching down in front of him. The fingers that had sealed his lips are now busy at the zip of his trousers. In a moment, Max's head tilts back in an attitude of simultaneous resignation and satisfaction as the woman's head begins to slide back and forth in front of his crotch.

'I'm sorry,' says the real Max from across the real room that they are both sitting in, watching something that seems to have happened not just ten but a hundred years, a dozen lifetimes, ago.

'No,' says Amy, 'I'm sorry. It's me the one who should be apologising, not you.'

'I don't know what to say,' he says.

'You don't need to say anything. How – where did he get this?'

'I went back to the hotel,' says Max. 'Some member of staff found it on the CCTV camera from that night and sold it on to some – I don't know, some dodgy geezer. Somehow it ended up on – this.'

The images are still rolling and Amy, though she is still clutching the remote control, is powerless to switch them off. She closes her eyes.

'I was drunk,' she says. 'Though obviously that's no excuse. I—' She closes her eyes again, unable to look at him, unable to look at anything.

'You don't have to explain anything,' says Max. 'I was there, remember? I knew what was going on. And it doesn't excuse anything. It doesn't excuse me.'

'One last adventure,' she says, choking on the words, feeling the bile rise to her throat.

'Don't. Don't beat yourself up over it.'

'It's just—' She gags, fighting for breath, feeling the tears well up in her eyes, fighting them back to stay adult and sane about it. 'I can't bear to think that Colin—' She can't finish the thought, not out loud. 'How did he get hold of it? Why did he have it hidden away?'

'I don't' know,' says Max. 'I don't know. I tried to find out. I tried to track down how it'd got in the hands of – whoever. How it got from A to B. It's one of the reasons why I never wanted you to see it. Because I don't have an explanation. Maybe the only person who can explain it is Col, and it's too late for that.'

The tears are rolling down Amy's face now, but she is silent. This is her bed – she shouldn't make a meal of it. The clash of clichés in her head almost makes her laugh and she tries to wipe the tears away with the back of her hand, but they keep on coming.

'I'm sorry, Max,' she says again. 'I should never have done that. Not to you. Not to your brother. I'd forgotten about it. After all these years – '

She looks at the screen one more time but the image has gone. Without her noticing, the scene has been replaced by another one as sordid and stolen as the last, two men this time, one reaching into the fly of the other in what looks like some squalid basement. She's missed the new caption.

'I'll destroy it,' says Max. 'I should've destroyed it before I'd ever watched the damn thing.'

'No.'

'You shouldn't torment yourself with it.'

She quickly presses a button on the remote, switching it off. The system reverts back to the television, the noise of some moronic show filling the room, and she kills it quickly.

'Can I keep this?'

'What?' says Max, astonished.

'I'd like to keep it. Please.'

Now it's Max's turn to not know what to say. He decides the topic needs turning, but she can see he doesn't know where to turn it to. 'Karen's coming over this weekend,' he says at last.

'That's good. How are the wedding plans?'

'Still on track. We'll see when she gets here.'

'Max, I hope this doesn't sound too awful but I'd like you to go now.'

He gives her a sad, puzzled look, the kind a pet dog might give its weeping owner. 'Are you gonna be all right?'

'I'm gonna be fine.'

After Max has left, Amy picks up the remote control and sets the tape going again from the place where it stopped. The tears have dried on her cheeks now, though the light from the screen still reflects off their tracks as she watches the two men in the shadowy, indistinct basement whose intimacy has been pried upon by the unblinking eye of the hidden camera. It's all very tawdry and reprehensible and none of it is very clear but she knows, just as well as she recognised her own wedding-night dress in the previous clip, that one of the men she is looking at is the man she met yesterday; that the hand reaching eagerly inside his sexual partner's trousers is Craig Sefton's.

45

The light here is special. Right now, here, at this time of the day, at this time of the year, the sunshine on the trees and the mountains and the river, even in the timid genteel reaches of a dying afternoon, is special beyond special.

She wondered if they'd be here still. The last time she was here their future looked decidedly unbright. But she's collected the coroner's report now and paid to have it translated into English, not wanting to rely on her own dodgy French to know what it says. Not that she didn't known already what it was going to say. An untimely leap; the meeting of a head and a log. She had expected no surprises, no recriminations, and so were there none.

She took the train down – the Eurostar to Paris then a domestic line to the nearest station and a taxi from there. Winston is in Europe at the moment too. They talked about travelling down together but in the end it proved impractical. He had a jazz festival to get to and she had a wedding to avoid. It was cool. While Winston was chilling out to Herbie Hancock somewhere in Belgium she was keeping her distance from a bunch of people who wouldn't have wanted her there anyway, but whose happiness she can't bring herself to begrudge.

After long deliberation, Amy destroyed the video tape and deleted Colin's dossier on Craig Sefton from his laptop. She still doesn't know where Colin got the tape from and she doesn't know why he kept it hidden. He may have seen the scene from the wedding party footage. She will never know for sure whether he did or he didn't. She likes to think that he kept the tape purely for the information it contained about Craig Sefton, and that the other part had escaped his attention, but that too she will never know for sure. The reason he had it and how he came by it – all of that died with him, and that's the end of it.

But the thought that through the long years of their marriage together he might have known and not said—

It's still a thought she cannot complete, and she knows now that it always will be.

Before she came away, Amy went to talk to her GP, Dr Anand. She told him about the fox, how she thought it had spoken to her in the voice of her husband. Dr Anand listened patiently, before asking her what she would like him to do. He could refer her to a psychiatrist, if that was what she wanted, but what she was going through sounded like a hypnopompic state.

'I'm no expert, but if you imagine the moments before you fall asleep and your consciousness begins to fizzle out, it's like the real world dissolving into the dream world. This is the hypnagogic state. The opposite is the hypnopompic state, when we're waking up but our mind is still clinging to the dream. In times of stress, such as losing a spouse suddenly at a young age, the mind can be drawn into such a state so that it doesn't know whether it's awake or dreaming. Have you seen the fox lately?'

'No. Not since – Not for a while.'

'Then I wouldn't waste my money on a psychiatrist,' said Dr Anand with a smile.

All the while, as she looks back at the road that's brought her here, she is being kitted up. She keeps a lookout out for Patrick. She's never forgotten him, with his blue flight suit, long hair and student beard. The Club Elastique de France, 1989, going headfirst into the water up to the waist. It sounds silly now that she thinks about it. How else is one to bungee-jump into the water other than headfirst?

While she's being weighed and measured and her ankles are being bound in the carabiners and the safety harnesses are being fitted, she looks up from her feet and sees him walking down the line of waiting sacrifices. As he gets closer he glances across to see who's being prepared and she notices him do an obvious double-take.

'Hello, Patrick,' she says as he walks up to her.

'Amy.'

He recognises her – he remembers her name. She feels flattered until she recalls what he must've gone through since Colin's accident – testifying before the inquest, worrying about his livelihood, a job he clearly loves passionately. She almost apologises for the hell of it all, then thinks she's done enough apologising recently for one lifetime. Those apologies were for the old lifetime. The new one shouldn't need them.

'What are you doing 'ere?' he says.

She sighs. She isn't sure what to say. She isn't sure she needs to say anything, it's such a fine day.

'I didn't go down the last time, remember?'

Patrick seems at a loss for words at first. Amy senses a conflict in him between wanting to say the right thing, the words he thinks she will expect from him after all they have been through apart, and wanting to fly in the face of conformity. Finally he settles on an understatement she might well have selected herself in his place. 'I got the impression you might 'ave been – put off for good.'

She smiles. She feels the need to smile suddenly, to show him she hasn't come back looking for some crazy mad-woman revenge.

'To be honest with you, Patrick, I don't know why I came back. Maybe I'll explain it to you when I see you down there.'

He smiles back at her but quizzically, not yet satisfied. *Perhaps later*, his expression seems to imply.

She shuffles out onto the tiny platform at the edge of the bridge. Yes, her thoughts are flying, just as they were flying last time when the car swerved to avoid the dead fox in the road. Possibly they're even flying beyond the speed of light but that isn't enough anymore. She looks out at the sky around her, at the low hills on the horizon beyond where the river alters its course and passes from her view. She can feel herself shaking at her own fear, at the possibility of the unified life stretching before and after the drop.

'OK,' says the man with the hand on her shoulder. He pats her on the back. 'Good to go. I'm going to count down from five.'

'Count from three,' she says.

'Trois . . . '

Amy spreads her arms, ready to dive.

'Deux . . . '

She bends her knees.

'Un.'

In one breath, she pushes away from the bridge and launches herself defiantly at the sky gods. As her feet leave the platform, Amy Trent gives herself over to reality.

Available from Armley Press

Coming Out as a Bowie Fan in Leeds, Yorkshire, England
By Mick McCann
ISBN 0-9554699-0-2

Hot Knife
By John Lake
ISBN 0-9554699-1-0

Nailed – Digital Stalking in Leeds, Yorkshire, England
By Mick McCann
ISBN 0-955469-2-9

How Leeds Changed the World – Encyclopaedia Leeds
By Mick McCann
ISBN 0-955469-3-0

Blowback
By John Lake
ISBN 0-9554699-4-7

Speedbomb
By John Lake
ISBN 0-9554699-5-4

In All Beginnings
By Ray Brown
ISBN 0-9554699-6-1

Leeds, The Biography: A History of Leeds in Short Stories
By Chris Nickson
ISBN 0-9554699-7-X

Reliability of Rope
By Samantha Priestley
ISBN 0-9554699-8-8

The World is (NOT) a Cold Dark Place
By Nathan O'Hagan
ISBN 0-9554699-9-6